Books by M K Scott

The Talking Dog Detective Agency
Cozy Mystery

A Bark in the Night
Requiem for a Rescue Dog Queen
Bark Twice for Danger
The Ghostly Howl

The Painted Lady Inn Mysteries Series
Culinary Cozy Mystery

Murder Mansion
Drop Dead Handsome
Killer Review
Christmas Calamity
Death Pledges a Sorority
Caribbean Catastrophe
Weddings Can be Murder
The Skeleton Wore Diamonds
Death of a Honeymoon

The Way Over the Hill Gang Series
Cozy Mystery

Late for Dinner
Late for Bingo (December 2018)

The Ghostly Howl

By

M K Scott

Chapter One

M AX STARED OUT the window at the passing scenery, which consisted of long stretches of fields. The occasional irrigation equipment stretching across the rows of produce like a metal praying mantis signaled they weren't in the city anymore. His nose hit glass, repeatedly, no doubt trying to smell the area. The German Shepherd grumbled and turned to his owner and driver, Nala. "I'll miss the burger festival. Every burger known to man and dog-kind in one place. Bison burger, turkey burger, prime rib burger, and, of course, cheeseburger!" He finished with a strong upswing of his baritone on his favorite burger.

Most dogs loved going places. Max did most of the time. Nala not only was blessed with an enchanted rescue dog who could talk, but he was also very observant, which made him excellent at finding information. He was a great asset in the private investigator business. His awareness of his environment had a downside, though. He believed what he was told until his nose or other senses told him differently. A recent radio broadcast had two foodies talking about a burger fest in downtown Indianapolis.

"They weren't even talking about this week."

"Sez you."

"I do." Nala eased off the gas as the vehicle in front of her slowed. It was obvious by the position of the people in the car ahead that they were arguing. The bad thing about passing those engaged in fighting while driving was they could be just as erratic as a drunk driver. When the problem car slowed even more, Nala braced herself for the inevitable and swung to the left. When she cleared the vehicle, she could address her partner's concern.

She stomped on the gas, not getting much oomph for her effort. Her vintage beetle wasn't known for its speed surges. Everyone, including her best friend, Karly, who owned a beater of a station wagon, insisted she needed a new car. Too bad no one was handing out free ones. If she had all this extra money lying around, she wouldn't be driving the two plus hours for a job in Southern Indiana.

As if sensing her thoughts, Max asked, "Why are we taking this very long car ride to *New* something?"

"New Albany. I already told you why." She sighed, thinking in some ways Max resembled the most recent guy she dated. It only took two dates to decide that Max and the no-go guy had similar traits. He didn't listen that well to her, either, and he also liked cheeseburgers. She'd expected more on the listening front while they were at the getting to know you phase. His phone got more attention than she did. Nala might have even let the relationship go for a few more dates if her business partner, Sawyer Donovan, hadn't said something when her date showed up at work. Sawyer recognized him from a disability case he'd investigated previously. It worked in her favor. She was looking for an excuse that wouldn't have everyone declaring she was too picky when it came to men.

Her driven, businesswoman mother had no place for slackers in her heart, while her police captain father didn't tolerate liars. More importantly, Karly, her friend who helped run the local shelter, was already suspicious of the man because he didn't have a dog companion or even want one. Max hadn't met the man, which was intentional on her part. She pressed her lips together, ready to put that sad episode behind her. It was sad because she'd projected on the man what she wanted him to be, and it wasn't the first time she'd made that stupid mistake.

"Well?" Max inquired with a cock of the head. "Tell me again. I'm a dog, not an elephant. Dogs aren't known for their memories."

No need to point out to him all the videos posted online of dogs greeting their service member-owners with great enthusiasm after being separated for years. "We're going to help out my old friend, Regina. She has a family emergency."

Max barked several times as a car passed them with a dog in the back. "Sorry. Instinct and all. I thought you said your friend was going to London. How is that a family emergency?"

Well, he *had* listened, which gave him one up on her previous date. "Regina's sister won a week's vacation to London. Unfortunately, it wasn't something she could schedule at her convenience. It was for some sort of event she had to go *now* or not at all. Regina is her plus one. Even now, they're already on the plane, whisking their way across the pond. We'll be staying at her house with Teddy."

"Who's Teddy?"

A beeping came from the radio, a crackle, and then an Amber Alert. "Ashlee Boden, seventeen, vanished Saturday, the thirteenth, around ten pm. Ashlee was wearing jeans and a red University of Louisville hoodie. She has blonde hair, blue eyes, and is five feet, six inches tall. Anyone who has seen her or has any knowledge of her disappearance, please contact this number."

The station gave the number while Max talked over it. "That's a *real* case. We should go find Ashlee. So, what is it *we're* doing now?"

Cute. He assumed he was helping. The only reason he was coming along was that she couldn't think of a reason not to bring him.

The green highway sign reminded Nala that she was only twelve miles from the exit where she'd get off and try to find her way to Regina's house—another reason why a new car with a GPS would be helpful.

"*I...*" she emphasized the word, "will be taking over creative writing classes for two days. Regina's college insists that the teachers find their own subs. They aren't fans of canceling classes, even for emergencies."

"She got you?" Bark! Bark! He smirked and lifted his dog eyebrows. "Do they know you're a preschool teacher?"

"Doesn't matter. I'm sure she told them I'm a licensed teacher. How bad could college students be?"

Max opened his mouth to say something but acted confused. Finally, he admitted, "I have no clue how bad college students could be." He stared out the window, and then said, "*Animal House.* I rest my case."

Well aware her dog enjoyed movies, she was surprised he had watched such an old one. "That was a movie. College students do not have food fights, especially considering how much university food services charges for a simple sandwich. Fiction. We talked about this. It'll be fine."

He gave a blubbery snort. "Once again, who's Teddy? Maybe

another chance for you to find the elusive one you've been searching for your entire life?"

"Have you been watching the Hallmark Channel?"

"Guilty."

"Teddy is Regina's cat."

"I love cats! I love chasing them and making them hiss. Gotta love how they arch their backs and spit."

The stay wouldn't be that long. Besides, Regina told her Teddy had no issues with dogs. "Be on your good behavior. Not our house, not our cat."

He winked. "You know me. I'm always on my best behavior."

She sucked in her lips, trying not to laugh. Canines were a great deal more sensitive than most people knew. Her dog never had an unspoken thought, she knew a great deal about how easily he could be offended. Hopefully, he could manage at the house with Teddy. She was sure the dog would not be welcomed at school.

The directions her friend had given her led her straight to the cottage half-surrounded by woods. The place was almost in a nature preserve, which made it very quiet. It would be a change from her nosy neighbors and having to explain away Max's behavior or any overheard remarks her canine might make. No one would believe that her dog spoke. His often outlandish views on life, dating, and cats were attributed to her.

The sun was sinking behind the pine trees when they pulled into the long driveway, leaving plenty of time to unpack and go over the lesson plans. The students probably wouldn't even notice the change in teachers, considering all older people tended to look and sound alike to the younger students. It hadn't been that long since she'd been in college. Only the unusual prompted a second look, depending on the time of day. A professor could be dressed up in a gorilla suit and only get a yawn in an early morning class. While an afternoon class, with a young, handsome professor sporting a fedora and an over-long scarf reminiscent of Dr. Who, might get more than a few females to sit up in interest.

Personally, she figured most would assume she was Regina, they both had similar builds and hair coloring. Maybe she shouldn't mention she was subbing at all. If she did at the start of class, many wouldn't hear her anyway. Those who did might even use the information to skip class. They'd slide out while she turned her back to write their assignment on the whiteboard. Regina warned her that *could* happen.

The house door had a keypad lock. Nala tapped in the code. Inside, cut flowers were scattered across the foyer and broken glass, which must have been the vase that held them. Had someone broken in? If they had, should she enter? Where was Max?

Her backward glance located her dog doing a sniff survey of the yard. "Max!"

A muffled "Busy!" drifted up from her dog's location.

Not what she wanted to hear. Sometimes she wondered who was the dominant one in their relationship. Unfortunately, she had the suspicion it wasn't her. She slapped her leg. "Max, now!"

He lifted his snout from the leaves and gave her the look that announced his sentiments better than words ever could. The leaves crunched under his paws as he loped to the door. Once on the step beside her, he lifted his head and stated, "You rang?"

Sometimes it was hard to decide if she should be irritated or amused by her dog. Her lips tipped up. "I did. I think someone may have broken in to the house."

Max took a step back. "Call the police."

It would be logical. Still, she wrinkled her nose. What if it were nothing? She would look foolish to the local law enforcement officials in an entirely different county than her own. "Get in there. You're a dog, and it's your job to ferret out wrongdoers."

He gave his head an emphatic shake. "That part is highly over-rated. Remember the last time you ordered me to bite the kidnapper?" He grimaced, then stuck out his tongue. "Yuck! Yuck! Yuck!"

"Point made. No biting this time. Just a quick look around to see if the culprits are still here."

Max inched up to the door and sniffed. "Cat. Big cat."

"How can you tell if it's a big cat?" Sometimes she was pretty sure Max made this stuff up to sound impressive.

"In the hallway."

"What?" She turned quickly to see a creature the size of a very furry beagle glaring at them. Nala pulled the door shut without thinking.

"Smart." Max nudged her. "I would have done the same thing if I had hands."

She dug her phone out of her purse. "I need to check on some-thing." A few taps brought up the information she needed about the creature inside the house. She might as well read it aloud for Max. "The Maine Coon Cat is the biggest of the domesticated cats. It can be forty-eight inches from tip to tail and weigh as much as thirty pounds."

"Cowabunga! That's an animal I'd like to avoid."

Just in case her dog wasn't getting it, she added, "Teddy is a

Maine Coon Cat."

Max glanced at the closed door, then up at her. "Ah, you're telling me we're supposed to live in the same house with that prehistoric creature?"

"Yes." No need to tell her skittish pup the cat might not be in the best mood over his owner's departure, demonstrated by the smashing of the glass vase. Cats could be moody. "I imagine he'll be lots of fun once you get to know him better."

"Yeah, that's what they said about Godzilla, and you remember how that turned out."

Nala placed her hand with the phone in it against her chest. "I keep my promises. I'm going in. I'm just surprised you're afraid of a little, tiny cat. I wonder what the dogs back home would say if they knew a cat frightened you."

"I know what you're doing, trying that backward psychology on me. It's not going to work. That isn't a cat. It's more like a dozen cats sewed together. That means it has the same disgruntled attitude of a dozen or so cats. It's a nightmare come to life. No, thank you. I'll stay out here. There're so many nice smells I haven't fully enjoyed. Leave your phone so I can call the ambulance if needed."

"Be a coward then. I imagine real-life police dogs would have no problem entering the house. Just think. They take down robbers, terrorists, sniff out drugs and bombs, and even find trapped people after earthquakes."

Max's head went down as she named all the things brave dogs did. Finally, he snapped his head up. "All right, I get it! Brave dogs get the job done. Open the door and let me show that cat who's boss."

Nala opened the door, and Max sprang through the opening.

There was a clatter of nails, a feline screech, a woof, and then another clatter of nails as Max vaulted out of the door opening.

"Okay. Teddy is the boss. I'm going to sleep on the porch."

Chapter Two

STUDENTS MOVED SLOWLY down the tree-shaded paths between red brick buildings to reach their early morning classes. A low-lying fog hugged the ground making the buildings appear to be hovering on a cloud as if in a futuristic movie. Nala yawned and consulted her map about which building she should be in. A large X marked the humanities square. Figures that it would be the one farthest from the parking lot. Oh well. She'd remember that detail on her next teaching day.

"Hey!" Max bumped into her leg for attention. "Ever notice how much the students resemble zombies?"

Some moved silently on a mission, but the majority were staring down at their phones and somehow navigated with a type of sonar that kept them from bumping into things. Not far from her, two phone watching students bumped into each other. It was a system with definite flaws.

As for the one creature who shouldn't be talking—*was* talking.

"Hush!" She hissed the word. "You know the rules."

It wasn't her idea to bring Max. It was probably against protocol. After a night of crowding her in bed and murmuring in his sleep about a demon cat, she knew she'd have problems leaving him alone today. What she didn't expect was no sign of her canine when she rolled out of bed. After calling and calling, she had to leave to arrive for her class on time. Inside her beetle sat Max in the passenger seat. How he managed to open the door without thumbs baffled her. His stance and straight-ahead stare announced he would not be moved.

Technically, she outweighed the dog. Even still, when he decided he didn't want to do something, she couldn't move him. It was like he had Velcro on his paws or had an internal magnet sticking him in place. She had no time for a battle she'd lose anyhow. Instead, she drove to the university and tried to decide on the way how to handle the situation.

There would be no leaving him in the car. Max had taught himself to roll down the windows, but none of the students would expect that, and some might feel the need to break the car windows to save the dog. Her lips pursed as she pondered her lack of options. Elvin, her friend and sometime work associate, devised a guide dog vest and harness for Max. His original intention was to use it to pick up girls who would feel sorry for a blind man. It hadn't worked as well as he'd hoped and ended with a woman's boyfriend tossing him out of the bar.

Still, she had used the harness and vest when investigating and donned a pair of dark glasses to complete her disguise. Ironically, people dismissed blind people as witnesses, but they were so much more aware because they depended on their other senses. As a pseudo-blind person, she had all her senses and the benefit of people trying to ignore her. Early on, when she chose to use the harness and the glasses, she discovered people would practically run to get out of her way. Every now and then, she'd get an unasked-for helper who would walk beside her and narrate the entire stroll down to the cracks in the sidewalk and the weather. Hopefully, she wouldn't have any of those today.

When they got closer to the building, she slid on her sunglasses, hoping they'd be dark enough to hide her eye movement. Inside the building, she found her classroom and the door was unlocked. All was good. She laid out the outlines she'd prepared for the students. Regina mentioned they could also download the outlines online. Some teachers included the notes online, but Regina didn't, pointing out it gave students just another reason not to come to class.

That sounded so much like her friend. Normally, Nala considered herself a rule follower, but she was a slacker in comparison to her friend. Quite frankly, Regina would never have a non-guide dog attired as if he was. Then again, she wouldn't have a wild animal in her home masquerading as a domestic pet. To be honest, though, Teddy, the cat in question, had been welcoming to Nala.

The outlines were on the front table, and she had the upcoming due date written on the board before the students entered. Knowing better than to greet them with a cheery good morning as she would her pre-school students, she stood off to the side and watched them enter. Max laid behind the desk and was, for all intents and purposes, hidden, which worked out well. Her sunglasses hid any interest she might display in the students' antics.

A few walked to the front table and picked up the project outlines. Most sleep befuddled individuals slipped into a seat and opened their computers or stared at their cell phones. It was hard to miss the slender earbud cords attached to the phones, especially when they were in neon colors, making her wonder how the student could possibly hear. Regina probably would make some general announcement about the class beginning, then march around the room reminding anyone who wasn't complying.

Just the possibility of doing so had Nala wincing. No way would she do that. So far, adults were much quieter than preschoolers, especially in the early morning. There was some slurping of coffee, which made her regret she hadn't brought some to kick-start her system. The search for Max this morning had cut out leisurely activities such as coffee and breakfast. All she wanted to do was get through the class and the one after that. She could pick up lunch on the way to Regina's office, which was, of course, on the opposite end of the campus. After a lunch break, she had office hours and wasn't sure how she'd handle that, since she had no experience with creative writing. She was, however, decent at reading. Her former students were considered primo if they mastered their name and the alphabet. Surely Regina didn't expect her to grade anything.

Two students were engaged in an animated discussion in the hallway. Their voices carried.

"No! She vanished. I don't know what happened to her."

"Weird. She didn't say anything to you? You know about her stepfather? She didn't like living with him. Called him a dictator."

A dismissive snort sounded. "What parent isn't. Besides, she's already accepted at Purdue. This first semester here was only to get a few of the general classes out of the way and a compromise for her mother. It cuts down on the expense, too. She was transferring in January. No, this isn't like her. At least they have an Amber Alert out for her."

"Not sure what good that would do if the ghosts have her."

If the ghosts have her? Nala wondered if this was code for a gang or something. If it was, it wasn't one she'd ever heard of. How intimidating could you be with a name like The Ghosts, which implied you'd be white and hovered above the ground. One of the students, a bespectacled girl, stood and walked to the door and closed it. Her actions ended the conversation that had Nala speculating if her unknown speakers had been discussing the same girl they'd heard about on the radio. Oh yeah. *Class.* She was supposed to be teaching.

"As you can see by the date on the board, your next story is due by October twenty-sixth." Nala started with what she thought was the most important. She scanned the students to see who was attending. None were looking at her. At best, she saw the crowns of the heads from her standing position as they peered at their electronic devices. A few were even typing on their keyboards, but as far as she could tell she'd said nothing requiring *that* many key-strokes.

A hand went up in the back. She acknowledged the male with a nod. Oops, a blind person would not have seen that. So much for that disguise. "Yes?"

"Will this class be canceled for Halloween?"

Nala sucked in her lips. She'd expected some questions she might have trouble answering, but she assumed they'd have more to do with crafting a story as opposed to holidays. As far as she knew, Regina had a liberal holiday package with both Christmas and Thanksgiving off. There was Labor Day, too. She couldn't think of anything else. The Fourth of July occurred in the summer and some of the other holidays occurred on Sundays, which would normally be off.

She assumed any partying could be done after class and asked, "This is a morning class. Why would you need to be off for Hallow-een?"

The boy shrugged his shoulders, having no real answer. Fortunately, she had consulted her notes. A blind person would not be reading off a paper—or at least a non-Braille surface, not that the act would serve her anymore. However, so far, no one had even bothered to look up except for holiday boy.

"Today, we are going to discuss the power of observation."

Door-closing girl cleared her throat. "On the outline, it mentions characterization."

Really? This was how it was going to be? She'd read the notes thoroughly the night before while Max trembled beside her. She couldn't be sure how much was actual canine fear and what percentage was acting.

She steepled her fingers together and gave the girl a tight smile. Her father always advised playing to her strengths. Observation *was* her strength. "You're right. The outline does say characterization. We should know about your characters via their actions. Instead of saying Kevin was a jerk…"

"Hey!" One of the male students exclaimed while the others giggled.

She should have known there would be a Kevin in the room. Undeterred, Nala continued, "…it is important to show why Kevin is a jerk as opposed to saying he *is* one. Maybe he put American cheese slices underneath a friend's windshield wipers on a hot summer day."

This caused a few interested looks, making Nala grimace. Could be there would be some blurry windshields on campus in the upcoming days. "He could have broken up with his girlfriend via text or social media."

Another male glanced at Kevin and shook his head. "It's like she knows you."

It was probably time to give Kevin a break. "Little things say a lot about a person. For example, you could have two people meeting for a meal." She hesitated. She had gone off the notes but had fifty more minutes to fill. Two people having a meal reminded her of her last online match. Great material to show total weirdness in a few actions. "Maybe they don't know each other well. It could even be a first meeting, or it could be they've known each other for years. The important thing to remember is the reader doesn't know them. You're going to have to show the reader who they are."

Door-closer girl's hand went up. "How would you do that? Everyone eats when you go out for a meal."

"You'd assume that, maybe. You have a woman who refuses to order anything but an unsweetened iced tea. What does that tell you?"

"She's watching her weight..." door-closer girl answered.

Another voice called out, "She's paying her own tab!" earning a few laughs.

"She could have already eaten," an older woman suggested.

A few more answers were called out showing that the students were actually paying attention. "Now, keep in mind, you don't tell folks at the beginning of a mystery who the killer is. It goes the same for everything else. You drop clues along the way, hinting at how a person is without saying it outright. Never say someone is good or bad—show it. Do you understand?"

Halloween boy's hand went up. Before she could recognize him, he spoke, "Do we get November first off?"

Door-closer girl answered for her. "No, TJ. You do not get Halloween off or November first or the day after that. You actually come to college to learn something. Why don't you stop your idiotic questions so those of us who came to learn, can?" She turned and smiled up at Nala. "Could you give us another example please?"

Even though it was tempting to point out that her pithy little speech showed that door-closer girl took the class very seriously, she didn't. Regina wouldn't thank her for riling up her students. Best to go back to the memory of her most recent online date, which had the merit of being very short.

"Okay, you're back at dinner with two strangers who are on a date."

Someone called out, "How can they be on a date if they're strangers?"

"Online dating," Nala answered, giving the group a slow survey. "Most of you are unaware that currently you are surrounded by people your age, often in the same socio-economic group, even with similar likes since you're in the same elective class. It's like you're in a river of possible dating options."

Several of the students smiled and a few elbowed each other as she spoke. "Outside this world, it's often hard for people to meet each other, and they resort to a computer program to find an appropriate date in the surrounding area. Still, they're unsure of the process and watch the date for hints about who he is. We are the readers watching this date unfold.

"At the restaurant, the man gives his order explaining his food should not touch. He wants no gravy on his mashed potatoes and no dressing on his salad. What might his date take away from this behavior?"

Her top teeth sunk into her bottom lip as she realized her slip.

She meant to say what would the *reader* think about his actions. An older woman held her hand up. Nala nodded for the woman to proceed. If the students noticed the sunglasses, they might assume she was trying to be hip. They also might think she was a vampire and couldn't be exposed to strong light, too.

"I'd tell that woman on the date to run fast. He can't even fake normal for a first date or even worse, he has no clue what normal looks like. He sounds like my ex-husband. It took me twenty years to unload him."

"Ooookay…" She lengthened the word, not sure if the class was turning into an impromptu therapy group. Obviously, she was right to refuse the possibility of the second date. With preschoolers, she had to schedule every minute, but adults would appreciate the time to work on their project. "Why don't you take about fifteen minutes and work on an opening scene. We'll discuss a few."

Someone murmured about Professor Collins never giving them time to work in class. Another voice hissed in a low tone to shut up. Nala pretended not to hear and glanced at her watch. Goodness, there was thirty minutes left in class, and she totally ruined her disguise. As if on cue, Max walked out from behind the desk.

What else could go wrong? Door-closer girl glanced up and squealed, "A dog!" She eased out of her chair and approached Nala. "Can I pet your emotional support dog?"

Her what?

The student angled her head to Max, whose ears were forward, catching every word, "I assumed he was for social anxiety. I mean, with the sunglasses and all, you wouldn't have to look directly at the students. Professor Collins mentioned to me that she'd be gone, and a friend would be filling in and would need some help." She held up both hands. "That's what I'm doing—helping."

That's not the word Nala would have used. "Go ahead, pet him."

Somehow, without intending to, Nala ended up explaining to the class that she was a private eye as opposed to a creative writing professor, although she did emphasize she had a valid Indiana teaching license. She explained how Max helped in investigations and summarized a few cases without using names.

Halloween boy held up his hand. Great. He'd probably want to know if he got Veteran's Day off. Nala had pocketed her sunglasses. She knew better than to pretend she hadn't seen his hand. "Go ahead."

"Maybe you could help find Ashlee?"

Before she could reply, Max did. "Yes!"

Nala quicky cut in. "Ventriloquism is another skill I use in an investigation." She could hear students moving in the hall. "Looks like class is over. See you next time."

Several of the students stopped by to pet Max. TJ, who she thought of as Halloween Boy, stopped by, too. "Are you going to be here all day?"

"I have a class after this one, then office hours." It made her curious about why he was asking. He didn't strike her as super studious.

He held up a hand as he left. "See you soon."

Chapter Three

A DISGRUNTLED MAN in a tweed jacket blocked Nala's exit from the classroom. He waved his index finger as if scolding her for piddling on the kitchen floor. Max, never a fan of such tactics, emitted a low growl.

"A dog! That's what I'm talking about. No wonder my students deserted my class to attend yours. It's hard enough getting the shallow creatures to write a decent sentence without texting abbreviations. Now I have to deal with a rent-a-cop and her flea-bitten mongrel!"

His full-throttle attack had Nala stepping back. It would be better to have some distance between them in case words failed him and he resorted to fisticuffs. "I, ah, didn't catch your name."

"Simon Ledbetter. *Doctor* Simon Ledbetter." He gripped the lapels of his jacket and puffed out his chest. "Perhaps you've heard of me. I've written several books."

"The name sounds familiar." A simple appeal to vanity usually soothed most ruffled feathers. Every seat in her last class had been filled, and there were even a few who leaned up against the wall. She made a conscious effort to stick to characterization, but a few of the students had heard that a private investigator was subbing along with her crime-solving dog. They came with questions. For a big group, they were mannerly and most signed the attendance paper she sent around. "Oh, I'm sure I've read at least one."

"Which one?" he asked with a smile, moving into a better mood, probably assuming anyone who read one of his books couldn't be all bad.

Sawyer Donovan, her office mate, warned her about her impulsive mouth. He liked to joke that he was the predictable one because he did most of his work using a desk and a laptop. He surfed social media sites to catch those enjoying disability checks doing skydiving and surfing while she usually had to do some legwork to solve her cases. Along with the legwork, she made up stuff to cover her snooping. Now and then, it bit her in the butt. It usually happened when she didn't have a clue what she was talking about. *Sorry* would have served her better as she made her way to the commons to grab a soda for her and a bottle of water for Max.

"There's so many. The name escapes me. Name them and I'll tell you which one." She stifled a sigh, hoping he wouldn't expect her to detail the plot line. It must have been Max's personal decision that the man wasn't a threat because he sat and yawned.

"Yes. Yes, there is." Dr. Ledbetter held up his hand. "There's *The Character Closet*," he folded down his thumb.

It was hard to tell if the book was fiction or a manual for acting. She wanted at least something she could say that implied she'd read something. She had nothing, so another finger went down.

"*Verbs That Like to Run With Wolves.*"

So far, the books sounded like textbooks. Dr. Ledbetter probably assigned them as the required books for his course and at eighty dollars a book, too.

The middle finger, "*The Uninspired…*"

"Loved it! Wow. You nailed it."

His brows lowered as he finished the title, "…*Teacher*. Strange. I would not have thought you'd have enjoyed my memoir. It's about, of course, the tedium of working in a state school with such mediocre students. I'd appreciate a review."

"Of course, I'll get right on it. It's time to take my therapy dog outside." *Aha!* She inserted that in nicely. What kind of person would he be to report her for having a therapy dog before she wrote the review. The verb book would have been a better bet. At least she knew something about verbs. Some were passive, others active, and there was one that never liked to be split from its significant other.

Informed of the plans, Max lurched to his feet and headed to the door. Dr. Ledbetter must not be an animal lover. He backed out quickly as opposed to petting the shepherd. Once outside, Nala circled the building to find a private spot for Max to do his business. She shook her head at the uncomfortable conversation. She reverted to her childhood habit of saying cookie names as opposed to cursing. It kept her in good with her mother, and it had stuck. "Snickerdoodles!" Half the time, she sounded as if she were eight years old when mad, or at the very least, obsessed with cookies.

"What now?" Max asked, then glanced around for eavesdroppers.

"Yeah. You *should* look around. This isn't a safe place to talk. These are the people who would believe in a talking dog. The same ones that walk in slow motion, certain that if they get hit by a school bus, they'll get free tuition. The office should be good. I doubt anyone is going to come by and ask me questions, which is just as well—I'd give them awful advice. How can I give anyone career advice when I don't have my own life worked out?"

"Dunno." Max's mouth dropped open. "Whoops."

Nala held up her hands. "Stop it! Stop it now!"

"Stop what?" A student stuck his head around a bush.

He possibly thought she was talking to him. "Oh, nothing. My dog tends to eat plants. I'd prefer he didn't. I don't always know which ones are not good for him."

The student made a derisive snort. "Use the leash, man. Show who's in control."

Max snapped his head around to glare at the student, but he was already gone. For that, Nala was extremely thankful. Despite her instructions for her pooch to keep his lips sealed, some things got the best of him. One of them was people treating him like a dog.

There was no reasoning with him on that matter. When a former owner's girlfriend enchanted him, which allowed Max to talk, his ordinary dog life had spun out of control. The girlfriend had made a hasty exit, leaving a chatty dog with a man who didn't even talk to his girlfriend. It didn't end well.

Now Max insisted on being called an *investigative partner* and at the very least, a *canine companion*. "Glad you ignored that jerk." She glanced at her watch. "Too bad all these pop-up conversations cut into my office time, leaving me no time to stop by the commons."

It wasn't like she expected anyone to come by with a burning question, but Regina had also left her a job along investigative lines. All the professors were expected to write a book a year. Occasionally, professors might work on a book together. It wasn't uncommon for a faster writer to hijack a premise for a book. It must be how a fiction writer, who labored over a book for years, felt when someone came out with a book with the same name one week earlier.

Regina had struck up an acquaintance with a visiting professor from Britain and wasn't sure if he was interested in her as a woman or in her book plans. She assumed that anything Regina wrote would be related to writing. Hopefully, it wouldn't be anything related to verbs and their social life.

First, she'd have to casually bump into the British guy, which required her being around the office. No one would bother introducing her, so she'd have to do it herself.

It felt like she had been walking forever. A quick consult with the map informed her there were two more buildings before she reached the teacher's office. Later, it would be a return trip to teach the third class of the day. Here she thought college profs had it easy.

An accented voice spoke, causing Nala to look over her shoulder at a blond man wearing wire-rimmed glasses.

"How civilized."

"Hello." She didn't know what else to say, but she had a feeling he might be exactly who she was looking for.

"Hello to you, too." He gestured in Max's direction. "Who is this handsome chap?"

Her dog's head went up, proving he was just as affected by flattery as the average person. It would be hard to get any information if Max started following the man around like a besotted middle school girl. However, he wasn't too hard on the eyes. His oxford shirt was uncuffed and the sleeves rolled up, which made it a touch more practical for the Indian Summer weather. His pale skin testified he hailed from somewhere with less sun.

"This is Max."

The man leaned over to pet the waiting shepherd. "Hello, Max. I'm David. I'm a visitor to this campus. I haven't seen you here before. I'll assume you're a visitor, too. Good to see that the campus is allowing animal friends on campus. It makes the place much more civilized and homelike."

"How so? I understand the homelike part, but not the other." She had heard some schools were allowing more therapy and guide dogs on campuses.

He chuckled as he straightened. "I almost thought the dog talked, but I assume Max would have a manly timber."

Not as deep as you might think. Nala gestured for him to continue.

"I'm not sure what the stories are around here. Back home, they expect kids to go a little wild when they go to school. Sleeping late, not keeping their room clean, and there might even be some rowdier activities. Those who arrive with pets have to keep more regular hours because their pets need to be fed and exercised."

"Good point." Gingersnaps! The guy was likable, which would make her possible opinion biased. What if he had a clue that she was an investigator and was trying to make her like him? Nonsense, there would be no way he'd know. All she'd have to do is work in pertinent questions. "Guess what?"

He merely raised his eyebrows, which may have been his version of guessing.

"My friend, Regina, I think you know her."

"I do," he agreed in that very proper British manner that was devoid of any emotion.

"She went to London. That's why I'm here, and you came

from…" She was going to say London, but that would be like assuming everyone came from New York.

"Cambridge."

"Anyhow, that's ironic. The two of you going in opposite directions. Why are you here?"

"It's an exchange program. As a fellow of the Theodora Program, we're expected to travel and see how various educational institutes work around the world. I chose this school at random."

So far, he didn't act like a book stealer, but then again, she could be prejudiced, due to him being nice to her dog. What she needed to know was if he had any need to write a book. "I was just talking to a professor in the English department that wrote a book called *Verbs Running with Wolves*." Nala was sure she had butchered the title but didn't care. "I hear professors have to write books all the time."

She put the tidbit out there to see if he'd take it. Instead of replying, he pointed behind her. TJ stood there holding hands with a diminutive female who didn't even look old enough to be in college. He grinned when she turned and yelled, "Max's owner and Max! We need your crime-solving skills!"

A sideways glance revealed British guy had caught the details. So much for being covert, now she'd just have to be clever. Being secretive was always easier.

Chapter Four

AWKWARD SILENCE ENSUED as Nala decided how to spin it for David. "Creative writing, ya know." She managed a dismissive smirk. "They probably want help on their latest detective story."

TJ shook his head hard, demonstrating he'd overheard her whispered aside. "You gotta help us find Ashlee before it's too late!"

"Please!" The petite girl begged, sealing the deal.

"I guess I'll take this in Regina's office," she announced to David, who appeared not only curious but a bit too avid for her comfort. It might do her well to set Max outside of the door, although she doubted if her dog would be willingly excluded from the conversation. Her canine would complain she might miss a valuable tidbit of information. The office key was in her pocket. The university might not be a fan of Nala using the office, but it was Regina's decision, showing she trusted Nala. Not only did she expect her not to ruin her classes, but to get the goods on David.

At the prospect of moving, Max surged to his feet, as Nala gave David a hopeful, backward glance. There was only one problem. She didn't know where Regina's office was.

"Ah, I was wondering…"

"Lower level. Seven A. It's right next to the office they gave me, which was vacant. I'll show you."

The four of them plus Max were practically a parade as they followed the path that led to the lower level entrance. They attracted some interested glances or more realistically, Max did. Many students were possibly missing the comradery of a family pet. TJ edged closer in turn, dragging his companion along and yammering as he did so.

"When I heard you're a detective…"

She held up her hand to halt the torrent of words that threatened to break free. She didn't need the details spilled in front of David. The man might start investigating her as opposed to the other way around. "Remember, client confidentiality. We'll talk once we get in the office, where I can take notes."

That stoppered TJ, but it had the opposite effect on his friend. "As a detective, couldn't you just arrest the culprit? I know it's her old boyfriend, Cody. He didn't like her going out with other guys. Ashlee vanished when she was with another guy. That proves it!"

It didn't prove anything. The new boyfriend could be just as liable or even more so since he was on the scene. She held up her hand once again hoping it would have a better effect than previously. "Office, please."

The young woman sucked in her lips and acknowledged she'd heard. David, on the other hand, wrinkled his nose as he commented. "Official police business. I feel like I'm smack dab in one of those crime dramas."

Exactly what she didn't want. "I'm not a police detective."

Nala needed to be clear on that part. People often confuse what detectives and private investigators do and use the terms as if they're interchangeable. While she could investigate a probable crime, the police usually didn't welcome her on the scene. Her trusty sidearm was in her messenger bag, but it was for protection only. Even if she had a burning desire to take out a bad guy, if she did so she'd be treated as a criminal, too. If she cornered a possible felon, she had to call on the local authorities to arrest and apprehend. What she did was all the deep investigation the local authorities didn't have time to do. She also took the cases often labeled as *events* as opposed to *crimes*. Vanishing family members, harassing phone calls, and money relocating itself into others' accounts were a few of the matters she handled.

The girl elbowed TJ and shot him an annoyed look. Obviously not what she wanted to hear. Oh well, it was hard to define exactly what a private investigator did without sounding too much like an obsessed ex-girlfriend trolling social media for information. The cyberstalking was more of her newest partner, Sawyer's, stock in trade. The man excelled in combing social media sites for pertinent information. As a gumshoe, she took to the streets for clues.

Their escort pushed open the door and motioned them in while he held the door.

What a gentleman! It was obvious why Regina was taken with the man. Not head over heels, though, if she thought the man might be out to steal her book idea. Apparently, in the button-down world of academia, intellectual theft was a rampant issue with successful con men excelling in creating a charismatic persona.

Max trotted slightly ahead of her with his head close to David's hand. The leash she attached to her canine companion was merely a fashion accessory. She never held it tightly, which allowed Max to walk slightly ahead if he wanted.

Most people liked Max, and he usually returned the favor with few exceptions. In all their cases together, Max had never taken to the criminal sort. They avoided him as much as possible, too. It was as if they both sensed something about the other. It could be the criminal recognized in the shepherd a type of dog used in sniffing out bombs and drugs. They could also be leery of his mouth full of sharp teeth. If they knew him like she did, they'd be more avoidant of his cheeseburger demands, smart-aleck remarks, and bad jokes.

There had never been a felon that Max had liked, but unfortunately, she couldn't always get Max in close contact with the suspect. His head was within petting distance of David's hand, suggesting David was okay. Was the man as guileless as he seemed, or was he a super criminal? Or could it be the act of stealing a book didn't register with Max as a crime?

They all filed into the narrow hallway crowded with mailboxes and delivery boxes sitting in front of various doors. There were plastic containers on each door. Some filled with papers—possibly student work, although Regina mentioned most work was done online. A few doors had whiteboards with magnetic markers attached for messages. Down at the end of the hall, a tall man dressed in a plaid shirt and a narrow tie conversed with a middle-aged woman garbed in a dowdy dress, sweater, and glasses hanging from a beaded chain. Mentally, Nala analyzed their clothing in regards to their jobs, a game she played to sharpen her investigative skills. Often, she had only seconds to decide if someone could help or harm her.

Since they were in the staff offices, she knew they could be professors. The man had the lean, angular, no-nonsense look of math, possibly computer science, or some type of engineering. The floral print on the woman's dress suggested a softer subject in the humanities, while the glasses suggested librarian and the reading of epic poems.

David stopped in front of an office with Regina's name on it. "Here we are." He angled his head back in the direction of the conversing two. "I saw your assessing look. What did your deductive skills tell you about my co-workers?"

This again? She often felt like a trick pony at the circus. If she got it wrong, people were disappointed. If she got it right, instead of being enthusiastic, people found ways to explain it away. She cleared her throat, ready to deny she'd been doing exactly what he'd accused her of. Instead, she said, "The man is in the math discipline. He tends to be abrupt and not exactly chatty. However, he finds it easy to talk to the woman because she represents everything he isn't. She's into the arts, specifically the humanities, possibly literature. By his stance, I'd say he thinks his discipline is more important than hers. The way he moved in front of her since our arrival shows a protective or proprietary attitude. He's cutting us off from her."

Even though she knew it was showing off and a bit of a reach, she added, "The woman knows the man thinks his job is more important. She knows better, but has chosen not to mention it yet."

"Bloody hell. You not only hit the nail on the head, you hammered it into the ground. The man is a physics professor who also teaches trigonometry. He's not social, especially with those in departments he considers beneath his, which is about all of them. With great surprise, I've witnessed the budding relationship between the *Physics Commandant,* as the students refer to him, and the British Literature professor, who is not only a sweetheart but has a mind sharper than a buzz saw and just as quick."

Good! She was right. For a second, she had doubts. She glanced back at the two, only seeing the man's back and a little flowered material peeking out on both sides of the man's legs. There was definitely a relationship there, but she decided on second thought it wasn't romantic. They both had offices here. It would have been easy enough to enter one another's office for privacy, although it could be they were trying to avoid the appearance of being an item. Mature love confused her. Who was she kidding? Any love baffled her. So far, she was batting zero when it came to her love life—never having had the experience of finding Mr. Right or even Mr. Good for Right Now.

Her eyes may have twinkled, knowing she'd made another correct deduction. It didn't hurt to have the admiration of an attractive man, either. *Down girl*! The Brit was Regina's property if she wanted him to be. As girls, they insisted whoever called dibs first on a male got exclusive rights to him, until she didn't want him anymore. At the time, most of their crushes were on boy band members and television stars, males they would never meet except in their fantasies.

Trying to turn the moment playful, she held up her index finger and blew on it. "Another one for me."

"Ha! It's a challenge, is it?" David pushed up his slipping glasses, hiding his expression.

She hadn't said anything about a challenge. What would constitute a challenge to an English professor? Would they write a paper on the situation? Meet at dawn and recite their favorite poems? The one who could correctly quote Shakespeare wins? Ah, how to answer? A challenge might keep her in David's company long enough to find out more about his propensity to steal other people's work.

Max might take a sudden dislike to him, settling everything. People put out an odor when they lied or tried to hoodwink another. And there were numerous sayings about things smelling fishy or not right. Some included the individual smelling *off*, too. At one time, people must have been able to sniff out deceit.

As she didn't have that ability, Nala deferred to her strong point: her observation skills. "Sure. What *is* the challenge exactly? I'm not clear on it."

He grinned. "Let me think of a worthy challenge. I'll let you know." He pointed to the door on the other side of Regina's. "I'll be close by. Come by and knock when you're through. I'm sure I'll have something by then."

He took a few steps to his door, and Max tried to follow. *Traitor.* "Heel."

Surprisingly, the dog sat and gave her a glare. He hated it when she treated him like a dog. Worse, the look David shot over his shoulder shouted *flirty*—in a geeky way. This was so not the plan. It didn't stop her hormones from calling an emergency meeting, though. She did her best to form a neutral expression as she returned his gaze, then unlocked the office door.

Sunlight streamed through the bare windows, highlighting a few dust motes dancing in the air. The tiniest aroma hinted that Italian food had been consumed in the recent past. Books crowded the bookcase. Several were stacked on the desk. There were even wobbly towers of books on the floor. An empty square on the desk free of dust was where Regina's laptop must have sat. On the top of a short pile was a picture of Teddy, her cat. Max glanced at the picture and whimpered. The great pet standoff, she would handle later.

There were extra chairs in the office beside the rolling desk chair, but they, too, were covered with books. She moved the books and waved her impromptu guests to the chairs. As they sat, she closed the door.

"Thanks for seeing us…" TJ started.

"I know something horrible has happened to Ashlee. You've got to do something! The police blew it off. They mentioned college students vanish on their own all the time. Usually due to partying or hanging out with a boyfriend and forgetting to mention it. The officer went so far as to add sometimes the missing person decided to go to New York City or LA to be a star. That's so not Ashlee. She's this super achiever. She skipped a grade, and isn't even eighteen. That's why her mom was able to get an Amber Alert. Her mother thinks…"

"Tawnee, give the woman a chance to sit down. She might need to take notes or something."

Or something. Nala added silently as she sat and pulled her phone out of her purse. "Is it okay if I record this?"

"Sure." TJ answered for both of them.

Tawnee, who had been so eager to tell all, suddenly became close-mouthed and threw a panicked look at her companion. "We won't get in trouble, will we?"

"Not sure. Why?"

Nala's instinct shouted there was more here than a girl just up and leaving. "Can you tell me what you're worried about?"

Instead of the girl talking, TJ did. "There's a house not so far from here. It's been abandoned for as long as I can remember. There're rumors that something really bad happened in it once. There's more than one story. It's a big Victorian with one of those widow's walk things. One of the legends mentions an engaged woman throwing herself off the walk when she heard her fiancé had died in a shipwreck."

The girl looked at TJ, then shook her head. "You didn't finish it. It turns out her fiancé's ship did crash, but he survived and ended up marrying someone else. The dead woman's ghost is an angry one, and she's not pleased when people enter her home. I guess that's why so many kids dare each other to go into the house. I've never gone myself. I got up to the fence and decided against it because it felt wrong. You know what I mean?"

That she did. "Yes. You said there were other stories."

TJ deferred to Tawnee. "You tell it. You're better with that kind of thing."

"Okay." Tawnee straightened in her chair. "None of the stories are good, which explains why no one ever bought the property. Evil just clings to the place. One tale involves a husband who suspected his wife was cheating on him. The police showed up after a neighbor complained about hearing shots. They found the home owner, his wife, and the owner's brother, all gunshot. It was never clear who shot whom. They only knew about the cheating because he'd confided in his best friend. It could have been a home invasion, but no one really accepted that explanation."

"Is that the final story?" Nala discounted the stories. No one she knew had ever prosecuted a ghost for a crime. Still, there were plenty of things she could not explain with cold, hard logic. Her father's constant reminder to check everything kept her asking even though she dismissed ghosts as a possibility. It was always good to know who the other people considered the possible culprit.

"No." Tawnee grimaced. "The last is the worst. It's all about some rich woman luring young girls to her house to bathe in their blood. I'm not sure if that wasn't the plot from a horror movie."

TJ made a face. "I don't believe that one. Someone got that off that eerie podcast about urban legends and stuff."

The fact he believed the first two stories surprised her, but they could have happened. "Tell me more about Ashlee and the night she disappeared."

Tawnee sighed and pressed her hand to her chest. "We argued. Not a whole lot, just a little about her going out with Wyn. He's a risk taker. What's that award thing they give out for people doing stupid things before they accidentally kill themselves?"

Before she could answer, TJ did. "The Darwin Awards."

His answer proved there was more to TJ than being a class clown. The fact he was seeking out help for the missing girl demonstrated compassion, too.

"That's it." Tawnee agreed and continued, "I always thought we'd hear about him dying doing something stupid. I warned Ashlee not to go out with him. What type of a guy takes a girl to a haunted house on a first date?"

First date? How about any date? The possibility of being arrested for trespassing on private property didn't seem date-worthy to Nala. Then, there was the joy of stirring up dust and mice droppings combined with walking into spider webs. No, thank you. Still, these things may have been attractive to her when she was a teen. She considered it for a second, but still came back with a big *no*. "Why did she go? Was she really into this Wyn?"

"No. That's the weird part of it. I could even understand if she did it to make her ex jealous. That wasn't it at all. It was more to show Cody she could move on. It felt wrong. I told her not to go. I reminded her about the other girls who went missing. She laughed and told me that was just rumors."

"What other girls?" Nala knew her phone was recording but reached into her purse for a pen and pad. It paid to have back up notes.

Tawnee shrugged. "I don't know them personally. There were three or four." She looked to TJ for confirmation.

He held up five fingers. "Five if you include Ashlee."

"Five local girls are missing, and no one is investigating this?" That was an outrage. What type of town was New Albany?

Both TJ and Tawnee looked at each other as if trying to decide who would talk. Tawnee finally spoke. "I didn't know anything about it until after the Amber Alert, then talk started about other girls vanishing from the house. Some of the guys involved were afraid they'd get nailed for trespassing, underage drinking, and even kidnapping if the girl never showed up again. One did report his girlfriend missing, though."

"Super-hot blonde, too," TJ interjected, earning a frown from Tawnee, probably for the evaluation and not the interruption.

"Ellie. We knew each other. Went to school together. She was always in all these beauty pageants. Her goal was to become a star. It was never clear if she expected to model or act. I can see the police suspecting her heading to New York."

If everyone chose to lie about where they had been, it would be hard for the cops to follow a trail—if there was one left to follow.

"Did the cops investigate the haunted house?"

The two of them shrugged in unison as if they'd planned it that way. The cogs were already turning in Nala's head. Something wasn't right. She needed to find out who owned the property. If it was an absentee owner, he or she wouldn't have a clue what was going on. "Do either one of you have Wyn's number?"

Tawnee pressed her hands together in front of her. "Are you going to look for Ashlee? Did I mention we don't have any money?"

Of course, they didn't. Nala couldn't live with herself if she didn't try to find Ashlee. "It looks like I am. I always like a bit of a challenge to keep the skills sharp."

Never mind that was the reason she was barely managing to stay out of the red and taking substitute teaching jobs. How long could it possibly take? Could it be Ashlee was holed up in a cheap motel, trying to give someone a good scare? Even brainy girls could be dramatic now and then.

Chapter Five

EVEN THOUGH TJ and Tawnee expected her to go roaring out in search of their missing friend, she had a class to teach. What she *could* do to get things rolling was call Elvin. He would get her the information she needed without too much effort. After promising to keep the two apprised, she waited for the door to close behind them before making a series of phone calls. The first was Elvin, her friend and all-around tech guy who could find out anything. She never asked how. The knowledge of such techniques might cause her to object to his methods and dry up the flow of information.

Still, she'd known Elvin since high school. He might get close to being on the edge of the law but would never knowingly step over it, especially considering he knew her father was the Indianapolis Police Captain. He'd consulted on cases with her before and even eaten dinner with her parents.

Her last case paired him up with his former girlfriend. Since it was the middle of the day, she shouldn't be interrupting the newly reunited couple.

The phone rang once before the voicemail picked up. "It's Elvin. You know what to do. Beep!"

Voicemail. She audibly sighed into the voice. "Elvin. I need you now."

"That's what all the women say." He chuckled into the phone.

Typical. She would have thought being in a relationship might have curbed his questionable humor, but it hadn't. "Elvin. I thought I had your voicemail."

"You got me, sweet cheeks. What can I do for you?"

She wanted to insist she didn't always call for something, only she usually did. "I need you to look up some stuff for me. I'm in Floyd County, Indiana. I need any missing person reports on missing girls around the age of eighteen or nineteen."

"I've been right here. I had nothing to do with it. I'm reformed. I'm dating a woman near my age now."

She rolled her eyes. It was part of Elvin's schtick to make outrageous remarks before getting to the subject at hand. After working several cases together, she'd learned to ignore it. Her eyes tracked Max as he sniffed around the office. A tower of books tumbled over from his attention. She wasn't all that sure what her pet thought he was doing, until something gray streaked across the floor causing her to squeal and Max to bark.

Elvin's voice was loud in her ear. "What's going on?"

"It's a mouse."

"Are you up on a table?"

"No, I'm *not* up on a table. I'm sitting in Regina's academic office, and I didn't expect a mouse." A thought occurred to her that made her grimace. "Brownies! Mice chew on books and she has a few thousand in her office. I'll need to do something about it."

"Get a cat."

She was about to tell Elvin that it wasn't that simple, but it was. Regina *had* a cat. Mice would be quaking in their boots with the

Maine Coon nearby. However, getting Max and Teddy into her Volkswagen Beetle at the same time was another thing.

"Back to the information I need. There's an abandoned house that the local teens swear is haunted.

"Woo ooo!" Elvin managed a pathetic ghost impersonation.

"Very funny. The deal is the house is vacant and on private property. It has several gory legends attached to it, too."

"Do tell."

"Maybe later, after you get me the information I need. Right now, I need to know who owns the house."

"Address?"

"I got it. You'd be proud of me. I found it by looking up local urban legends online. One site specifically gave the addresses for each site. It's called—"

"Check It Out Yourself."

"How did you know?"

"I've used the site on more than one occasion." There was the sound of finger tapping on a computer keyboard. "Okay. I got the website up. Scrolling down to Floyd County, which surprisingly has a lot of haunted houses. Ah, here's an especially bloody legend. A Victorian on Morning Glory Lane."

"That's the one."

"No problem. Anything else?"

Nala replied, "Since you'll be digging through reports, why not see if the police have been called to that house."

"Here's an idea. Why not ask the police yourself, since you're already there?"

She made a dismissive snort. "If I thought it would do me any good, I would. At this point, the police tend to think missing college girls is a sign of too much partying. They might not have said it in those exact words, though. There has to be a reason for the police to believe the girls are not in peril."

"Obviously, you have no Officer Goodnight or a man in blue ready to do your bidding. Girls' parents?"

"Good question. Most parents would make a stink. I know at least one had an Amber Alert put out. I need to contact the parents, too. I might even find out they've heard from their daughters but haven't passed on the info."

"So, what's the dealio? Same old?"

Most of the time Elvin spoke a language based on old films spiced with what she assumed was 1940s gangster jargon. "Explain."

"Why are the kids going to the house?"

"Oh. I think a beer too many, and they dare each other. Since they are underage drinking and trespassing on private property, they aren't too keen on owning up to it. I have no clue what they told the police, if anything. Most were probably afraid they'd be blamed for the disappearance."

"They *could* be guilty."

"Yeah, I did consider that."

"I'll look for the missing girls report, but don't flip your wig if I don't find any."

She had no clue where he came up with these expressions. "What are you inferring?"

"Ah, Little Grasshopper is getting better and got the upswing in the master's voice."

Not only was Elvin good, he was cheap, too. It was her mantra that kept her from yelling *Get on with it!* "Go on."

"I might find all these girls aren't missing. You might have one missing and all of a sudden everyone has a story about their friend missing, too. It makes them into a mini-celebrity by tying into whatever is current."

Yeah, she should have thought of that. "It's a possibility. My daddy taught me to turn over every stone before I formed a theory."

"Right he is. I never want to get sideways of Captain Bonne. You can tell him that for me, too."

"Please. You know my dad already loves you. He credits you with saving my life on the first case." Actually, Nala kind of felt she had it under control, but she did appreciate the blue cavalry that Elvin managed to whip into action. "I need to call Sawyer, so I'll let you go."

"I see. I'm shoved aside for the blond dreamboat."

"Yeah, yeah. Sawyer is my office mate, and I need to check on what's happening at my office. I'll call you later."

"Keep telling yourself that, sister."

Elvin hung up before she could reply. Typical, but he was good—and cheap.

Chapter Six

S HE APPRECIATED BOTH Sawyer's expertise in navigating social media to find out needed information and the fact he split the rent. She'd paid her rent a year in advance when she previously received a big check from a client. What Sawyer paid for his share after he moved in was pure profit. It helped, tremendously. Still, she didn't know how she felt about her handsome co-worker. If he were more her father's age, she'd regard him as just another guy and possible mentor. The fact he wasn't even thirty, good-looking, and personable caused her best friend, Karly, to tease her relentlessly about romantic possibilities.

The phone burbled in her ear as she firmly pushed aside any reflections on his soulful eyes or skin that should be in cosmetic ads if men ever decided to wear makeup outside of Hollywood. Of course, with Sawyer's skin, he'd never have to resort to cover up or foundation. The ringing stopped.

"Hello?"

Sawyer. He hadn't answered with Bonne Private Investigations. Even though they discussed putting his name into the title, he deferred, mentioning he didn't know how long he might be there. It sounded reasonable at first, but if he answered the office phone with a simple hello it wouldn't do much for her business. Anxious daters who called for a background check would hang up, assuming they called the wrong number and would decide to forgo the date. Worse, they could go on the date without proper investigation and disappear forever. She really should speak to him about his phone greeting. "Ah, Sawyer."

"That's me."

"I wanted to check on how things were back at the office."

"Yeah, I know. Elvin just texted me."

Well, that explained the greeting. She couldn't remark on it, knowing he knew she would call. "Typical. I just talked to him, but you know that."

"Uh-huh. Not much happening around here. Without you and Max here, this place is dead."

"No phone calls?"

"Wait." There was the sound of rustling. "Your mother wants to know if you're going to be back in time for Sunday brunch."

Weird. Her parents knew she was out of town. Better yet, why would her mother not call her cell number? "I don't know. What did you tell her?"

"Pretty much the same. Told her I'd pass on the information. She then begged me to come over. She wore me down, so *I'll* be brunching with your parents on Sunday."

It also explained exactly why her mother had called. Her mother was a hopeless matchmaker. Gwen Bonne's first words when Nala informed her she had a partner, were to ask if he was single. Then, she showed up at the office, unannounced, with coffee and pumpkin muffins. Of course, her mother came to check out the new guy. After a few obvious questions, she winked at Nala and mouthed the word *nice*. Only, she may have only thought she mouthed it, because Sawyer blushed, grinned, then busied himself by moving papers around on his desk.

"Have fun. Be discreet. My mother could give the CIA lessons into interrogation techniques. She'll want to know the details of my cases and what all."

He gave a lazy chuckle. "Please. I have parents. I know the drill. I know nothing about your cases. So, how is it going? Should I ask, especially when I need to say convincingly 'I don't know anything' with a straight face?"

"I trust you. When in doubt, ask my father about his newest K-9 training project. He'll hog the conversation, and my mother won't get a word in edgewise." She smirked, imagining the look on her mother's face. "My teaching gig has turned into a *Twilight Zone* episode. On the way down here, there was an Amber Alert for an older teen named Ashlee. Runaway was my first thought. When they get older, it's not like the non-custodial parent is going to wrestle them into the car."

"Could be bribed with promises of a car or more freedom."

"There is that. Don't know much about Ashlee, except her friend is convinced she did not run away and thinks the ex-boyfriend had something to do with her vanishing."

"You know this how?"

"That's where the car went off the road—figuratively speaking." Nala hesitated, not wanting to admit that somehow, she started talking about being an investigator and her cases in a creative writing class. She wasn't a hundred percent sure how the subject came up, but it had to be her. None of the students knew she was a

PI. Talking about the business was not the epitome of being discreet. However, she didn't name names and some of the cases she used came from television shows. Still, Sawyer had been an insurance investigator longer than she'd been in the business, and her goal was not to appear a bumbling rookie. "I may have mentioned I was a private investigator."

"Somehow, I don't think that was in the lesson plans."

"It wasn't." Nala bit her bottom lip as she searched for a reasonable way to present it. Originally, she wasn't even going to mention it. Now she had to make her actions reasonable. "It was Max."

The dog in question glanced up abruptly. "Thanks for throwing me under the bus!"

It hadn't been her intention, but it made sense to her. "The kids were asking about Max. One kid asked if he was my emotional support dog. It made it sound like I couldn't go anywhere without him."

"Why would you?" Sawyer's voice sounded in her ear. It sounded like something Max would say, but her pooch had gone back to a sniff inspection of the room.

"You know. Restrictions against pets." Max lifted his head on the last word, causing her to clarify. "Canine companions and assistance animals."

"Well, he certainly qualifies as the last. Give the ol' boy a pat and a dog treat for me. I miss him."

Figures. He missed Max, not her. They'd barely been gone a day. If he said he missed her, while it might make her momentarily happy, it could weird out their working relationship. Another clatter of books and a small cloud of dust followed by a frenzy of barking meant another sighting of the irritating rodent. Date bars! She'd have to do something about the mouse. Maybe it was a pet. She discarded the idea as soon as it came. Mice were opportunistic and moved inward when they could. It was probably making a nest out of Regina's various, well-loved books.

"What has got Max so upset?" Sawyer asked.

Not willing to reveal that Regina's office was mouse infested, she decided to sidestep the subject. A wall clock revealed that her calls took a little longer than she planned. The walk back to the classroom would take a good twenty minutes, especially if she had to stop whenever someone wanted to pet Max, and there would be plenty. "You know how dogs are. They bark at anything."

Max, who had stopped barking, shot her an affronted look, which meant she'd hear about it later. Folks might think women held grudges, but it was nothing compared to Max, who remembered every perceived grievance. She'd deal with it. "Sawyer, I've got to go. I have another class."

"Try not to give away any trade secrets," he chuckled.

She had to admit his amused laugh did cause a warm sensation, even though his sense of humor kept her from melting. It sounded like he might be spending too much time with Elvin. Couldn't begrudge the man. He knew so few people in town. "I won't. I'll stick strictly to the lesson plan."

"You do that. I'll talk to you later. Have fun. Bye."

Nala stared at the phone. He hung up before she did. Even though she was ending the call, she should hang up first. The person who ended the call held the power in the relationship. It must be true since that particular bit of information appeared in a popular magazine. Oh well, she had plenty to do other than competing to see who could hang up first.

"Let's go." Nala nodded at her dog.

"Now you're ready. Haven't you heard me warning you about furry invaders?"

"I did notice you wrecking the place. Looks like I'm going to need to bring in Teddy to solve this mice problem."

"That monster! Why would we need him?"

Max somehow missed the obvious. "Cats catch mice."

"Ha! Lean, hungry cats catch mice. The best Teddy could do is accidentally step on the poor sleeping creature."

Rather than answer her dog, especially when he was probably more right than she wanted to admit, she picked up her purse and notebook and headed for the door. She swung her door open to reveal David, who was ready to knock.

"Just checking to see how you're settling in."

His lovely British accent made her feel as if she were in a romantic comedy. Too bad she didn't have time to probe the visiting professor to see how far he'd go when it came to stealing book ideas.

"Good, ah, I have to go to class."

"Cheerio. See you and your wonderful canine tomorrow?"

As far she knew Regina didn't work tomorrow. It wasn't on the schedule. "I don't have another class until Wednesday."

He cocked his head and gave her a flirty look, worthy of any diva worth her salt. "I wasn't talking about class. You're new here, and so am I. We could hang out, as you Yanks say, and grab lunch."

Neon warning lights flashed in her mind. This man was Regina's potential Romeo. It would help if she could talk to the man and get a feel for him, but she didn't want him to get the wrong idea. Still, she'd only be here for a week. "I could meet you for lunch. Any place in mind?"

"Splendid. There's a Mexican place on Plum Tree Avenue. They have outdoor seating, so you can bring your friend along."

"Sounds great." It really did, but right now she had to keep her focus on the work only. Never mind that the sight of his grin made her heart beat a little faster. Nothing would come of it. He could be a book stealer and was out to sweet talk her. That's all.

"One o'clock."

"We'll be there." She waggled her fingers and turned to check that the office door was locked before turning left to head outside.

The late afternoon sun highlighted the scarlet and golden leaves heralding the season change. No students were on the walkways, yet. The trees provided some shielding, too. As the day went on, most of the day students would leave, only to be replaced by the older evening students, who had a regular job and managed to squeeze in night classes in an effort to improve their lives.

Max must have noticed the lack of eavesdroppers also. "I like that guy. He may talk funny, but he is one of the few who shows me the proper respect."

What was it about your dog liking or not liking a person? Something about dogs were better judges of people. Realistically, Max loved every male in her life including Harry, who shared the office building, her father, Elvin, and Sawyer. Anyone who showed him the appropriate amount of attention earned his approval.

"I love the way David talks. As for liking him, I do, too, which makes things complicated."

"How so?"

"Regina likes him."

"Oh." They walked a few moments in silence. "Why can't both

you and Regina like him?"

"That's where it gets complicated." She shrugged. "Doesn't matter, we'll be gone in a week."

Chapter Seven

THE AFTERNOON CLASS had somehow heard about her crime-solving dog. Even though she gave the class their assignment and wrote it on the board, she had a feeling many would fail to do it. Once Regina returned, a few would swear it'd never been assigned, while the rest would keep silent. This routine also had occurred whenever she had a sub when attending school. Most teachers knew better than to expect homework. It was always hard to know who was responsible for the lack of homework—the sub or the students. Sometimes the teachers resorted to assigning a particular student as a go-to person for information. Once, as one of the assigned students, Nala had buckled under to peer pressure and managed to say no homework had been assigned on that particular day because there were so many after-school events and the regular teacher must have forgotten.

The memory of the incident made her wrinkle her nose. For just a brief second, she was popular with everyone. Then they remembered who she was—the rule follower, the honor roll student, and the daughter of a cop. Like tended to stay with like and her group was not popular. They tended to do the homework for the popular kids. Not her, though. Even though she enjoyed that brief moment of popularity, she wasn't willing to go against all she'd been taught.

Besides, she'd witnessed the snowball effect, too. Once you started doing one kid's homework, there was an entire line wanting you to do their homework and the answers had to be varied so no one would get caught, which seldom left time for your own work.

A few students appeared on the sidewalk, hushing any conversation she might have with Max. A couple even smiled in her direction. They were probably the ones who would have helped the popular students if an online business of selling essays and term papers hadn't sprung up. Regina had revealed that the university had purchased a service that scanned submitted essays and determined if they were original or plagiarized. This all happened automatically when the students submitted their work in an online drop box.

At one time, she might have considered cheating a bit of a crime. Since then, she'd witnessed much worse things. Nala decided the cheater only cheated himself. Technology occasionally worked for criminals, but people like Elvin used the same or better technology to track, then trap them. Thank goodness she had the man on her side. They reached the parking lot and spotted the beetle. Max did her the courtesy of waiting to voice his feelings until he was seated inside the car.

"I'm starving. Let's hit the drive-thru."

They did need to eat. Fast food wouldn't help with her resolve to get in better shape, though. What about all those people she saw running with their dogs? They were in great shape. The only time she ran was when someone behind her had a gun and was shooting at her. When that happened, Max was usually much farther ahead.

"Hate to say it, but your idea sounds doable."

"Woo-hoo!" His exclamation turned into a long howl.

"Please! It's a small car. I've told you before no howling in the car."

Max dropped his head and muttered, "Might as well say no happiness is allowed."

Drama queen. Used to his theatrical behavior, she chose not to reply to his histrionic display. Instead, she contemplated where they should go. "We need someplace that has fish."

"Fish! I don't eat fish. That's cat food!"

"Exactly. It would be nice to get Teddy a treat."

Max was almost at a loss for words. "Are you crazy? He gets a treat for terrorizing us?"

"He didn't exactly terrorize *me*. True, he was a bit grumpy. Consider this, we are strangers invading his home. He could be protecting his territory and out of sorts because Regina is gone."

"It's more like he's out for blood."

"Try to see things from his point of view. How would you feel if you were left alone while I went somewhere, then some unknown person showed up with a cat in tow?"

Max shook his head vigorously. "That would never happen. If it did, I would have to be dead and didn't make it to the pearly gates."

She started the car, reversed it, then put it in first gear as she tried to remember any fast food restaurants on the way to Regina's home. "You're not good at empathy."

"Impa Thee. Is that a game? Never heard of it."

"Figured as much."

The neon signs directed her to a familiar restaurant where she used the bargain dollar menu to order Max six plain cheeseburgers. She ordered herself a grilled chicken sandwich and tried to convince herself the chicken was much healthier than beef—even if it wasn't exactly a leafy green salad. When she ordered the fish, Max made a derisive sniff.

He probably was jealous of Teddy. In his early life, he had been rejected hard by owners because of his ability to talk. One owner even chased him from the house, declaring he was a spawn of the devil. Even though she thought she had taken good care of Max, he probably always watched for her showing another animal affection. Instead of seeing it as a natural affection for all animals, he saw it as competition. They pulled up to the second window to wait. When the employee handed over the bag, Max licked his chops.

The teen worker chuckled. "Better watch out or he'll wolf down your food."

Nala merely smiled in reply, unwilling to confess the majority of the food was for him.

They got to the edge of the parking lot before Max commented. "You didn't say anything when that jerk implied I'd steal food."

"Pick your battles. Hard as it might be to believe, I can't disabuse everyone of their dog stereotypes."

If she tried, she'd attract more attention than she wanted and might even earn the label of crazy dog lady. A private investigator walked a thin line of being unmemorable. They worked best if they faded into the background. Having a large, black German Shepherd with her, made it harder to blend in. Thank goodness more businesses were allowing emotional support dogs to accompany their owners.

The ride home wasn't that long, but she ended up unwrapping a cheeseburger for Max, unwilling to listen to his whining.

Anytime he continued to beg, she usually caved. That probably meant she'd be a lousy parent, who always gave in and bought her child candy at the grocery. However, she'd try to negotiate a deal with her hypothetical child. The fact she was trying to work out compromises with a non-existent child did not bode well. Not everyone should have children. It could explain why she wasn't married with a pair of ankle biters yet.

Women didn't have to immediately marry anymore. It wasn't the 19th century. A woman could live a fulfilling life and never marry. Nala had a full life with her job, friends, and family, but every now and then, she'd welcome some male companionship. If she thought her preschool job offered little opportunities for finding single men, it was practically a meat market compared to the investigative world. Most of the men she came across were guilty of whatever who hired her suspected.

The car bumped into the driveway. The living room sheers twitched, then Teddy's robust body appeared, causing Max to whimper.

"He's watching for us. Probably has spent the entire day thinking of ways to torture us."

Even though she'd seen a ton of videos of cats bullying dogs on social media, she never thought her dog would be one of the bullied. "Max, you're twice that cat's size."

"Ha! You might need to get your eyes checked. The only creature bigger than him is Godzilla."

Nala rolled her eyes. She didn't really need a cat and dog war right now. It is what it is, though. "Let's start over. We'll offer Teddy the fish. Give him plenty of space. There are probably spaces more important to him. We can make this work. Think of it as a challenge."

Instead of waiting for an answer, Nala parked, swung the door open, and grabbed the bag of food. Max hurtled through the open door with a clatter of nails. He lifted his head and pranced to the front door displaying major attitude.

"Glad to see you're feeling better."

"I'm not. It's called acting. I've decided that a dog with my natural good looks should be in the movies or at least in television commercials. I imagine I'll have to demonstrate my acting skills. I call this courage under fire, which could be for a military film or a superhero movie."

This acting career was news to her. "Sounds great. You can pretend that Teddy is the villain. You have to outsmart him by pretending to be harmless."

"I can do that!" Max responded with enthusiasm and a huge doggy grin.

Let's hope so. Time would tell. They entered the house through the side door. Something fell in the next room making Nala wince. Teddy would wreck the place at his current pace. If this were his normal behavior, it would make more sense if Regina only bought plastic home accessories.

A furry head peeked around the corner as Nala unloaded the food, dividing it into three piles: hers, Max's, and Teddy's. Originally, she was going to put Teddy's fish in his bowl, but that might mean nothing to him. For all she knew, Teddy regarded the bowl as a magical creation that manufactured treats.

"Max." She interrupted a stare down between Teddy and the canine as she placed the fish back into a bag as a plan occurred to her. "I want you to deliver the fish to Teddy."

Max hung his head. "Do I have to?"

"Courage under fire, remember."

He rolled his eyes. "Gimme the bag."

She handed him the bag, which he carried in his mouth to the hissing cat who backed away. He dropped the bag and ran back to Nala's side. She was used to Max tearing into anything that smelt vaguely edible. Teddy's cautious approach to the bag surprised her. One furry paw batted the bag, scooting it across the floor a few inches. He waited a few seconds, glancing back at Max, possibly being suspicious of a stranger bearing gifts.

Her phone rang just as Teddy pounced on the bag. Not recognizing the number, she hesitated for a brief moment before answering.

"Nala Bonne." Because she used her cell number for business and personal reasons, she'd decided on just using her name as a greeting.

"You're the detective with the crime-solving dog, right?"

When in doubt, she dropped back to the manners her mother had instilled in her. "With whom am I speaking?"

"Tawnee. We met at the campus."

The memory of the petite girl who wanted her to search for her friend came immediately to mind. "Yes. I remember. You have any news for me?"

"Yes. I talked to Ashlee's mother, and she wants to talk to you. I got Wyn's last name and contact information, too. Are you ready?"

"Just a moment." Nala pulled a pen and paper from her purse. The fact she had to go to the same items private investigators had been using for centuries amused her as she tried to ignore the ripping noises that came from nearby. No doubt it would be another Teddy-generated mess. "Go ahead."

"All right. Wyn's last name is Samuelson. His number is 812…"

Her pen raced across the page as she recorded the information.

"I haven't talked to Wyn. We're not friends. Maybe you could get more out of him using an ambush approach."

It was hard not to snort at the suggestion. She didn't know her suspects, making everything an ambush interview. Sometimes she got useful information, other times, the person reacted with hostility or silence. Neither served her. "I'll do that."

"Super good! I don't mean to be telling you your business, but I really think you need to visit that house. That's where the girls keep vanishing from."

Tawnee's suggestion concurred with her own conclusion, although she was hoping to work through more legal channels if Elvin could track down the owner. As for the girl giving her unsolicited business advice, it was nothing new. She would have thought as a teacher she got more than her share of advice from people who never took an education class or sat through a long parent-teacher conference. It turned out everyone gave her advice on investigating, from her father to clients who wanted to tell her exactly how they wanted her to do her job. Unfortunately, they sometimes wanted someone between a secret agent and a hitman.

"I'm working on it. I'm waiting to hear back who the owner is." Some investigators would have held back information making the process sound mysterious. Nala had always been mostly upfront. Sometimes, when she didn't have anything to tell a client, she didn't call back until something surfaced. No one wanted to hear she had nada, especially a paying customer.

"It could be a ghost, too. An angry one. You might need to hire a ghost hunter or maybe a ghost whisperer. Someone who would know what to say and not make the ghost any angrier."

Ghost hunter? She didn't know anyone like that. Karly had a psychic friend who could see auras and tell people what chakras were blocked. That wasn't exactly a ghost hunter. It would probably cost a great deal to get someone like that, even if she knew who to call.

Before she could even rethink her actions, the words were already out of her mouth. "I'm not a local. Would you know someone like that?"

"There're some guys at college who started a ghost hunting group. They don't even charge as long as they can film the ghost hunt."

"Videotaping would be a no. Have they found any ghosts yet?"

"No." There was a pause. "They got close one time. In one of their episodes that they put up online, a picture fell off the wall."

It was obvious Tawnee thought ghost hunters were a good idea, but it reminded her of that movie where a trio of armed hunters were always trapping and zapping ghosts. She wasn't totally sure if it was possible or even if ghosts existed. "Well, maybe I'll just take a look around before doing anything definite about ghosts."

"I got it! My Aunt Belinda could help! She's not a professional or anything, but she knows things."

"Like where the girls went?"

"Ohhhh, I should ask. Usually, she can tell when a spirit enters the room. Sometimes she even gets messages. It's not all the time, not like that medium on television with the super long nails. I can talk to her. I know she'll want to help."

Brownies! One of the first rules of investigation was to involve as few people as necessary. The more people involved was in direct relationship to the element of surprise vanishing, usually along with the most likely suspect, too.

"I'm sure Belinda is very good at what she does."

"She is. I'll get ahold of her right away."

"I'm not sure if…" She stopped talking when her cell registered the call had ended. Nala stared at her cell as if it was the problem. "Second time today. I don't need a medium to chaperone me. Of course, that would depend on my actually traipsing through a haunted house."

Something fell in the distance. Both Teddy and Max had disappeared, leaving a tattered fast food bag. That wasn't good. Might as well go clean up Teddy's latest mess. Instead of barking, hissing, or falling objects, an ominous silence reigned. Not good. She had no choice but to search the house and deal with whatever she found. She came across another scrap of shredded food sack. Instead of using bread crumbs, paper served as Teddy's choice for leaving a trail.

She turned the corner and couldn't believe the sight that met her eyes.

Chapter Eight

THERE, IN THE middle of the living room on the oval rug, Teddy slept curled in a ball, leaning against Max, who had his eyes closed. The fish sandwich worked! Maybe she could hire herself out as an animal whisperer. "Perfect!"

One of Max's eyes popped open, and he grumbled low. "Do. Something."

"What?" No way was she going to take a chance of having her arms slashed to ribbons by waking the feline. As long as the cat was asleep, she could get some work done instead of cleaning up after Teddy. "You could sleep. Normally, half your life is spent snoring."

"This isn't normal, and I don't snore." His whispered reply swung up on the last word approaching a whine. "It would be like sleeping with the sharks. No one does that."

"I'm not sure sharks sleep." Obviously, her animal whisperer skills didn't extend to maritime creatures. No need to point out her dog *did* snore. It wasn't like she'd be taking him to a sleep clinic.

Max cut his eyes to the large cat cuddled up to him as a loud, contented purr erupted.

Even though it was the last thing her dog wanted to hear, she said it anyhow. "I'm not sure he's asleep."

"I was afraid of that, and I'm starving. Where are my cheeseburgers?"

"In the kitchen. They will be there when the two of you are finished napping."

A heart-wrenching whimper came from her pooch as she turned to leave. She should do something. Knowing her dog, he would use this incident to squeeze out favors into infinity. There was only one thing she could do. In the kitchen, she grabbed the food bag, returned to the living room, and squatted beside the duo. She unwrapped a cheeseburger as Max salivated. She tore off a small piece, unwilling to shove an entire burger into her dog's mouth. Sure, it would be his preference, but he needed to slow down. He always ate like he was afraid food would be ripped from his mouth.

Max licked his chops as she lowered the food to his waiting mouth. *Swat*! Out of nowhere, a paw knocked the food from her hand. Max groaned as Teddy vaulted over the prone canine and inhaled the cheeseburger tidbit. Nala closed her eyes, tightened her hand on the fast food bag, and waited for the ruckus to erupt.

Nothing. She opened her eyes in time to watch Max lurch to his feet. There was a gleam in his eyes she seldom saw, determination mingled with outrage. The cat, unaware of the meaning behind the expression, approached the cheeseburger from which Nala had torn the portion.

A deeper voice than she normally heard from her canine came from Max. "Stop! Now!"

He inserted himself between the burger and the cat. Teddy ignored his words and reached between Max's legs for the burger. A claw caught on the paper, allowing the cat to draw the burger toward him. Max pressed his paw down on the burger squishing it before

Teddy could get it.

"Look what you made me do! I might as well eat road kill. I've had enough!" Bark! Bark! Bark! Bark!

It was probably more of the same in canine speak. Teddy flicked his tail a few times, then proceeded from the room with a regal lift to his head as Max wolfed down the squashed burger. Her dog looked up at the bag expectantly as she removed another burger.

Teddy and Max weren't best buds, but it *was* an improvement. Cheeseburgers, or the filching of cheeseburgers, appeared to be the tipping point. That she should have known. At least it would be easier living in Regina's house. Maybe Teddy wouldn't be so destructive. Nope. The sound of glass breaking in another room meant the feline had not stopped his destructive tantrums. Ginger Snaps! Her friend probably wouldn't have a breakable left when she returned.

It was as if an iconic lightbulb suddenly snapped on above her head. Sometimes that happened when she suddenly knew the answer to a case. This time, she knew what to do about Teddy. "I've got this. We gotta cat proof the place."

Max's head snapped up with part of a burger bun hanging out of his mouth. "Get rid of the cat. Hey! Great idea!"

The bun tumbled out of his mouth, distracting him. As he lunged for it, Teddy zoomed out of a dark corner and gobbled it up. No need to explain when actions spoke louder than words. If the cat was half the escape artist Max was, a crate wouldn't keep him contained. Because she valued her life, she wouldn't even try. No, she'd do the next best thing, but she'd need a laundry basket and a container of cat treats.

A few minutes later, she started upstairs shaking the treats and calling *kitty, kitty* in what she was sure sounded like a suspicious tone. She checked the bathroom. No cat and no niche large enough to hide a cat the size of a hefty toddler. She closed that door. Only a few more rooms to go, including the office and master bedroom, that had doors. If she could keep the doors closed, she wouldn't have to cat proof the rooms. Wherever he was, Teddy must be lying low.

A frenzy of barking let her know the exact location of a trouble-some feline. She closed the guest room before heading downstairs to gather up the breakables in the laundry basket and lock them up. How could she solve embezzlement cases and now be dealing with a wayward cat? If she could find the missing girl, that would add to her cred as an investigator.

NALA FOLLOWED TAWNEE'S jeep as it crept around the dark streets. If the college students were trying not to attract notice, driving under the speed limit would do just the opposite. Normally, cars that crept along the road were oversized sedans driven by tiny old ladies who could barely see over the dashboard. The vehicle in front of her, with its various bumper stickers promoting bands and a large marijuana leaf, would not belong to your average church lady. Any officer hiding in the tall weeds would probably follow the slow-moving vehicle, certain the driver was impaired. All she could do was hope they had some type of fuzz buster in the car similar to what Elvin had brought along on his impromptu visit.

She glanced over at her friend all dressed in black as if he were a jewel thief. "I'm not sure why you bothered to drive down. All your equipment is back in Indianapolis."

"Some of it," Elvin agreed with a grin. "How could I pass up ghost hunting? It's on my bucket list."

"Really?" A derisive snort accompanied her reply.

"Sure. Everyone has to do something that stretches their boundaries. So far, I've never been abducted by aliens. I have never seen a Yeti, Nessie, or Bigfoot. I did say Bloody Mary into a mirror three times. All I saw was my reflection. This might be my only chance to see a ghost."

A yip sounded in the back seat where Max currently sat. It was as close to a laugh Max permitted himself when others were around. She angled her head toward her dog. "See. Even Max thinks it's funny. There's no ghosts. It is just an urban legend like the hitchhiking prom queen."

Whenever some tale got repeated enough times you had people swearing it was genuine.

"Hey, that one *is* true, but she wasn't a prom queen–just a girl in a fancy dress."

The car in front of her picked up speed, forcing her to keep her eyes peeled for any sudden turns. It didn't stop her from teasing Elvin, though. Most of their relationship consisted of him teasing everyone else. "Did you pick the girl in the fancy dress up?"

"No, but Braeden, this dude I used to work with, his cousin did. Dark, stormy night and he saw her alongside the road."

A tale three times removed from someone she never met was *so* trustworthy. "Let me guess. He lent her his jacket."

"Yeah. How did you know?"

Nala held up her hand as the jeep's turn signal flickered to life.

They were going right. A quick glance in the rear-view mirror didn't reveal any headlights. Still, she debated about turning on her own signal. No reason to announce their destination. She'd turn with no signaling like half of the driving population around here. She made a sharp turn before answering.

"Was the girl hot?"

"Yes, she was. Hey, do you know Braeden?"

It was hard to believe someone as smart as Elvin could be fooled by a common tale. "I bet he came back to the house where he dropped off the girl the next day, only to have her mother answer the door and tell him she'd been dead for twenty years."

"Ha!" Elvin jabbed his index finger in her direction. "Shows what you know. He went back and there was a cemetery. He saw his jacket neatly folded on a tombstone with the girl's name. She'd been dead forty years!"

"Variations of the same story." She knew that Elvin knew that things changed each time something was told. That was one reason it was so hard for folks to trace their genealogy. Names, even countries of origin changed with each telling.

"You don't think there are ghosts, but you think your dog can talk."

"I never said that!" Never mind that Max could talk. A side glance revealed Elvin's furrowed brow.

"Okay. It wasn't you. I think it was Karly. So, you don't get psychic messages from your sidekick?"

The dog in question leaned forward and rested his head on her shoulder, possibly waiting for her response. Just in time, the jeep pulled over underneath a scraggly tree. An owl hooted as if on cue. All they needed now was a bat to slowly fly past the windshield.

"We're here," she needlessly announced as she parked behind the jeep.

Elvin pulled his black beanie down over his ears and handed a matching one to Nala.

She rolled her eyes at the offer of the hat but doubted he saw it in the dark. "My hair is already dark."

"True. What about spider webs and whatever else might crawl into your hair in an abandoned house?"

"Give me that hat!"

She tried to ignore her friend's laughter as she stuffed her hair into the knit cap. Max pressed his cold nose against the side of her neck as if asking where his hat was. For a canine, he could be squeamish about some things, especially bugs caught in his coat.

The car door creaked when she opened it, reminding her that the beetle would not last forever. Before she could get a foot out, Elvin leaned over and asked, "Why are we here so late?"

"We'd be more noticeable in the day. I tried to contact the absentee owner from the name you gave me. Unfortunately, all I got was some girl yelling at me in Swedish. I have no clue what she was saying. She could have been telling me it was the wrong number or that the guy had died."

"Tragically, inside the house…" Elvin used his spooky voice.

Max gulped audibly, resembling the cartoon dog who did likewise whenever danger threatened.

Elvin half turned to look at Max. "I swear, sometimes I think that dog understands exactly what we're saying."

You have no clue. Nala kept the thought to herself and returned to the earlier query. "Tawnee's Aunt Belinda, the medium, believes the dead listen or talk, not sure which one it is, at midnight or close to it."

A heavy-set woman in slacks and a colorful top appeared close to Nala's door. The crunch of fallen leaves would have alerted her if she hadn't been sparring with Elvin. It made her wonder how much the woman had heard.

"The veil between the two worlds is thinnest at midnight," the woman stated, which answered part of the question.

Elvin gave her a nudge as he climbed out the passenger side door. "That's what Nala was telling me. Isn't the closer you get to Halloween the better the reception?"

The woman gave a low, husky laugh that belonged in a low budget horror flick. "Yes. We prefer to call it Samhain. Anyone can get in contact with close relatives that have passed on. It only takes an open mind and a willingness to listen."

"Cool," Elvin replied with obvious enthusiasm. "Does that mean I can hear from my Uncle Ned? He's the one that got me interested in electronic snooping by letting me listen to the police scanner. Sometimes we would even go out to the sites where a crime was reported."

If Elvin ever dropped that tidbit near her police captain father, he'd get an earful about impeding police proceedings. She could thank Uncle Ned for Elvin's refusal to consider anything private, but then who was she to judge? She not only delved into people's secret lives but also used Elvin's services to help.

The silhouette of a shabby Victorian with a swaybacked porch stood near a couple of overgrown oak trees with bare branches that twisted and reached for the ground or possibly any trespasser. They reminded her so much of the malevolent trees that had come to life in *The Wizard of Oz* that she had to suppress a shudder. It sure was dark, especially after everyone turned off their car lights. The professional flashlight she bought on the investigator website gave out a strong beam of light, but it was narrow, which meant she could only see what was directly in front of her and only ten inches of it. Everyone knew that creepy monsters or the undead were usually behind you or secreted in the shadows elsewhere.

Snickerdoodles! Nala shook her head hard. Elvin's silly stories were starting to get to her. Besides, everyone knew ghosts couldn't hurt you. They might leave some cryptic message, but it wasn't like one would push her down the stairs. A glow of light illuminated the area as Elvin fiddled with his LED camp lantern.

"At last! I found a use for some of my camping supplies."

If there was less of an outdoorsman than Elvin, she couldn't think of one. The man had to have a wideband Internet hookup, plenty of outlets, and air conditioning to keep his electronic equipment at the right temperature. "You camped?"

The lantern allowed her to see Elvin grimace. "No, but I thought about it."

"Was it part of your getting back to nature stage?" She turned to let Max out before locking the car. No one knew they were there, and the location was very isolated, making her wonder what she hoped to lock out. Still, it was better to be safe than sorry. Some insurers refused to pay if your car was unlocked. No use taking chances with her cut-rate company.

He grunted, which translated to let's not talk about it. Ironically, when they started working together, they knew much more about the details of each other's lives. Nala didn't share nearly as much as

Elvin did, though.

Another light shone as Tawnee and TJ joined the group. With all their lights together, they should be able to brighten an average sized room. Victorians were usually known for their oversized rooms and no closets. The lack of closets meant nothing could jump out at them. On one of her school field trips, the guide explained that people then very seldom installed closets. They could be counted as an extra room and would be taxed accordingly.

TJ rubbed his hands together as he greeted everyone. "Ready to go? I got my EMF reader and a tape recorder. I can take video with my phone. It may not be expensive stuff, but if it was good enough for the *Blair Witch Project*, it should be good enough for this."

Her eyes met Elvin's, who gave a small nod. She wasn't sure if he was acknowledging the reference to a horror flick or was telling her to say nothing to dissuade the eager ghost hunter. TJ's friend must not have felt the same way. Tawnee placed a restraining hand on his arm.

"You need to be quiet, so Aunt Belinda can listen. None of that stuff you see on television where they're constantly stomping around. We don't want the neighbors to complain."

TJ made a slow circle, peering into the dark. "What neighbors? I don't see any lights."

"Maybe there's no close neighbors, but with everything that has happened, I bet the police are keeping a close eye on this place."

Nala found herself nodding. Even if the local LEOs didn't buy into the ghost story or the vanishing girls, they could still nail a few teens for trespassing and underage drinking. It wasn't exactly busting a crime ring open, but Nala imagined things were slow around here.

"With that in mind, we need to get inside. Right now, we're practically a searchlight where none should be."

A half-moon lent its light to the buckled sidewalk that the city never got around to fixing. No reason to if no one ever used it. When they walked past some overgrown bushes, something flew out, causing Nala to wrap her hands over her head. Most of the others jumped, but Aunt Belinda proceeded serenely onward as if on a Sunday stroll. Her head was cocked as if she were listening to voices only she could hear.

As much as she hated to ask, Nala did so. "You getting anything?"

The woman inhaled before speaking as she cautiously mounted the rickety porch that creaked and groaned with each step. "Weed. I can smell marijuana. Recent, too. Stale beer. Someone also made use of the bushes as a restroom. No wonder the birds were upset when we walked by. Obviously, they have nothing good to report on the previous two-legged visitors."

It didn't take a psychic to pick up the smells. Nala moved her wrist to allow the light to illuminate the path and prevent her from stepping in something extra icky. Even though Max was bringing up the rear, it was hard to see the black German Shepherd in the dark. Eventually, there was the rattle of nails on the wood porch, which she found reassuring knowing it was her canine. There was a nearby *hoot* that startled her. Apparently, the owl that greeted them when they got out of the car had flown in for a closer look.

"An owl…" TJ narrated, holding his camera phone up to capture an image of the feathery visitor, "is often a symbol of death."

"Of mice," Aunt Belinda added, unaware that the would-be ghost hunter was possibly making a video for online consumption. Since anyone could upload a video, everyone and his brother were cinematographers. They borrowed heavily from movies they'd watched and used copyrighted music until the video was taken down.

The psychic glanced over one shoulder in TJ's direction. "Oh dear. I didn't know you were making a video."

The sparkle in the woman's eyes told Nala she knew exactly what he did. This was not the type of medium she had expected. With both Elvin and her garbed in black, they looked more at home behind an Ouija board than the woman in front of them. Still, she knew better. Every now and then, her father had psychics volunteer information about missing children or where to find a corpse. Such information often ended up making them suspects, especially when they turned out to be right. It should have been enough reason to keep their insights to themselves. Oddly, those with the ability to see things others couldn't often felt compelled to help.

Right now, she was batting zero with the absentee owner and the new boyfriend, Wyn, who had actually run out the back door when she arrived earlier in the evening to interview him and his mother. Nothing said guilt like running away. Too bad she couldn't nab him for some private questioning. Besides being highly illegal, she had no place to take him. His mother was a little guarded but did reveal some information, believing Nala came from the university. To her credit, Nala didn't exactly say that. Instead, she *mentioned* working at the university.

The mother thought her son was up for some type of reward or scholarship. She babbled on about how her son enjoyed rocketry and spent a great deal of time at the local hobby shop. All that meant was he told his mother he was at the shop when he was really elsewhere. Just another twist on *going to do homework at the library.* That excuse must have gone the way of the dinosaurs with teens being able to locate needed information with a click of a mouse and never leaving home.

Back in the present, Belinda rattled the doorknob, which opened the door, the lock long since broken. It swung ajar with a creak, and she would have sworn a sigh, but that could have been Elvin crowding behind her. For an intrepid ghost hunter, he sure was walking close. Later, she'd kid him about it. It seemed fair. She'd heard his laugh at her fright about the bird flying out of the bush. Thank goodness she hadn't screamed. Private investigators didn't scream. They might cringe occasionally but screaming was out.

Aunt Belinda moved confidently ahead, which was amazing for a woman who didn't carry a flashlight. Moonlight shone through the bare windows highlighting the shabby furniture that belonged to another era and the footprints in the dust. There were plenty. Elvin's flash snapped as he took photos of the prints.

Just from looking, she could tell a number of people had gone through the place. Some had large feet, others, not so large. "Tawnee, would you have a clue what type of shoes Ashlee was wearing?'

The girl walked over and squatted to stare at the prints. She pointed to a smaller print with a logo inside of the footprint outline. "Ashlee has shoes like that. Right now, they're hot. Lots of girls on campus have the same type."

Elvin, who had been hovering over the prints, replied. "If half the girls on campus have the same shoes, then there's no proof she was here."

Yeah, she thought the same but saw no reason to slap the girl down. As an investigator, she often followed up on the thinnest of threads and often hit pay dirt. While Elvin saw the familiar logo as proof anyone could have been here, she had to go with Ashlee *could* have been here but moved on.

"What did Ashlee say when you talked to her last?"

Even though she'd asked a similar question in Regina's office, she decided to repeat it. People often elaborated each time they told a story, often remembering details they'd forgotten. As she waited, Nala took a survey of the room to find Max. The large dog shot past TJ who stood gripping an EMF reader in one outstretched hand.

A shrill sound penetrated the air along with a red flashing light. "It's a spirit…" TJ yelped and fumbled for his phone. The whine ended as suddenly as it began, leaving Max a little rattled as he sat close to her.

A spirit? Her top teeth worried her bottom lip. *That* would put a new spin on the case.

Chapter Nine

TJ HELD UP his phone in one hand and his EMF device in the other. He shook the device, which had gone silent. He muttered something about the unpredictability of spirits. Nothing there to speak of. Nala switched her attention to Belinda, who was an expert on such things. The woman wrinkled her nose and shook her head.

"No voices. Not even a good shiver as if someone walked over my grave." She cleared her throat, pulling TJ's focus off scanning the room for something ethereal. "You know those devices, while fun to use, can give off positives."

"Whadya mean?" The was a trace of suspicion in the student's voice.

It would be ironic if the sometime medium would spoil the game for the potential ghost hunter.

"EMF Waves are everywhere. You can find electrical lines by waving a monitor around."

The news didn't faze TJ, who held the device aloft and moved it slowly above his head as if seeking basketball player spirits, or maybe ones who liked to cling to the high ceilings. "There's no electricity in the place. It's abandoned."

That was the rumor Nala had heard. Otherwise, they'd just feel awkward using flashlights and lanterns. It would be curious to see how Belinda would counter the argument.

"It not just electrical magnetic waves that cause the reaction. All it takes is a large amount of metal to cause a spike. I saw a guy with enough jewelry to equal Mr. T who set a unit off."

"Mr. Who?" Tawnee and TJ chorused together.

When it came to old television series, Elvin was the expert. If Nala didn't stop him, not only would he explain who Mr. T was, he'd launch into his impression. "Anyone got a lot of jewelry on?"

There was a series of *no*. That didn't solve the random beep. "What were you doing when it beeped?"

"Looking at it."

No help there. "Anything else? Walk me through the moment."

"Ah…" TJ's gaze raced around the room, then came back to Nala. "I walked in after you. Tawnee's auntie was leading the way. I had the EMF monitor in one hand, and I was reaching for my phone with the other. They say you can take photos of ghosts, but you don't know it until you look at them later. Anyhow…"

When it looked like he might go off in explaining the principles of photographing ghosts, Nala circled her hand for him to speed it up. "What else? At the moment or even a little before it. Think!"

"I almost dropped my phone. Max came charging in here and bumped me."

Max bumping people was nothing new. People assumed that dogs had this sixth sense that allowed them to navigate. Technically, they were supposed to see better than humans, at least at twilight and dawn, when their primitive ancestors would hunt. Max, with all his bumping into folks, made a lie of that theory. He could even do it on purpose, which seemed more in character with the dog.

"Wait." Elvin held up his hand. "Don't you remember the collar I brought down with me?"

She did. It was the type of thing you'd see more on bulldogs or goth kids, a wide black stretch of leather studded with two-inch spikes all around. "I told you not to put that on him. It might injure him."

She shone her flashlight over her dog, exposing the massive collar. Belinda gave the collar a thorough survey. Patting Max, she said, "That could do it. TJ, why don't you test it out?"

A sullen expression replaced his earlier excited one as he stepped away from the door and waved the monitor in front of him. It remained silent until it got to Max's collar where it gave a long, sustained squeal.

"A dog collar! That doesn't even make a good story. At least I wasn't filming yet. It wouldn't add to my cred as a serious filmmaker."

A derisive snort escaped Elvin, who was probably thinking the same thing Nala was. Serious filmmakers didn't rely on cell phones as opposed to cameras. They also probably didn't depend on a rumored ghost to appear as opposed to hiring an actual actor. Why were they even bothering to trespass on what was obviously a questionable teen hangout?

The last thing she needed was to be slapped with a misdemeanor for trespassing. Despite the fact she was an adult, somehow her father would hear about it and lecture her. He probably put some alert on the criminal records files for her name, just in case. There was probably another for her mother. Knowing her volatile mother, he'd expect an alert more on her name than Nala's.

An arrest would also affect the possible issue of Nala going back to teaching if investigating didn't work out. No one wanted a preschool teacher with a record working with their darlings. Did the rest of the group share her concerns?

TJ had moved closer to the stairs, waving his ghost device while Elvin texted. Did he have an emergency that demanded he reply right now? More likely it was for his blog, *Hacker on a Mission.* Never mind, she'd mentioned several times that he couldn't use the details of the cases in his blogs. He passed off her remark by saying he changed the names to prevent any from ever making the connection. Instead of being Nala, she was Nina, intrepid investigator with a sassy attitude.

People could make the connection, but fortunately no one read his blog except maybe Elvin, his girlfriend, his mother, and Nala, the last searching for possible information leaks that could result in a lawsuit. To be fair, he had changed some of the facts. One blog detailed their search for Bigfoot, which had never been a case of hers.

Belinda had her arms folded and her eyes turned upward. It was hard to tell if she was communicating with the spirit world or just disgusted she'd agreed to come. Max kept close to her, making exaggerated high steps when he chose to move. The dust, debris, and whatever else on the floor bothered him. This was the same dog who left muddy paw prints through her entire home on more than one occasion. Sometimes there was no understanding him.

The only actual investigating came from Tawnee, who used her flashlight to inspect the floor inch by inch. She gasped, then squatted and reached for something on the floor. "It's Ashlee's earring!"

"How do you know?" If the shoeprint wasn't conclusive why

would an earring be?

"Oh, I know." Tawnee pushed to her feet and held up the earring. "I gave her the dolphin earrings for her birthday. The blue eye on the dolphin is her birthstone. I bought these when my family went on vacation to Key West. They're one of a kind. That's what the lady on the beach who sold them to me said."

Nala thought about saying something about the one of a kind remark, but she wouldn't. It would serve no purpose. As long as Tawnee hadn't bought them at the local discount store, there was a good chance it was the missing girl's. "Elvin, I need an evidence bag, please."

Normally, she carried her own bags, but her friend thought it would look better if she had an assistant, though she wondered how much an assistant would impress college students who weren't paying. Thank goodness he made a stop at the local convenience store for snack food and assorted size baggies.

Elvin pocketed his cell phone with a sigh. It was apparent he'd already forgot he carried the investigation backpack. He rummaged through the bag, pulled out a baggie, and a permanent marker.

She took the baggie, opened it, and held it out to Tawnee, who dropped the earring into it, even though there was no need to worry about fingerprints. Nothing could be obtained from the tiny section of earring. It was a French wire with a hook. Sometimes, she favored similar earrings. They didn't get lost as easily, which led her to the question of why this earring was on the floor.

Ashlee could have been in a hurry and failed to hook the wire in the clasp. After a few beers, it wouldn't be too farfetched to think Ashlee and her date got a little frisky. Males who didn't wear earrings weren't always careful about them. Wyn could have been running his fingers through her hair and caught it. There could also have been a struggle, the reason Wyn vanished out the back door.

She needed to locate Wyn. He might think he'd ducked her, which worked in her favor. When he wasn't expecting it, she'd pop up, along with Max, and hit him with the hard questions and hope she'd catch him unaware. So far, most of the cases she solved weren't cracked because of ambush interviews, but due to long hard searches, usually involving money, sometimes paper, and the occasional social media gem. People had to be totally unaware of who read their posts.

After closing the bag, Nala noted where it had been found in black marker, then handed it to Elvin, who eyed it, then placed it in the bag. Now what? She'd established Ashlee had been in the house with a ton of other people. Not exactly a discovery, but more of a confirmation that this was where she told her friend she was going.

Tawnee nudged Nala's arm. "Do you think someone took her?"

A sudden boom was accompanied by the tinkling of glass shards. Max barked, and everyone else froze except for Belinda, who spoke in a deep voice unlike the one she had used earlier. "The spirits are here."

Fig bars! What spirits? She stared at Belinda, realizing by the lack of reply that she hadn't verbalized her thoughts. "What spirits?"

"The ones who live here." Even in the dim light, it was easy to see Belinda's arched brows that announced it should be obvious what spirits were here. They certainly weren't the spirits that jumped in when they stopped at the jiffy mart for gas. "They're not happy."

Even though she was tempted to ask if spirits weren't generally unhappy and stuck around as opposed to proceeding to the light, she didn't. If whatever broke was the warning shot, then the spirits had a great deal in common with Teddy. Maybe there was a spirit of an oversized cat in the house.

"It's not an animal spirit," Belinda relayed the fact very matter-of-factly. She inhaled deeply, then proceeded. "I can feel a pressure on my right side, which indicates a male.

The hairs on Nala's arms stood up. Communicating with the spirit world had not been on her agenda. Curiosity overcame her apprehension to all things spectral. "Who is it?"

"I'm not sure. I don't always get names. Usually, I don't. It's a man. A tall one in old-fashioned clothing." She stopped and placed a hand to her ear. "What's that? All right. I understand." She gave a little nod, as she carried on a one-sided conversation. "Yes, yes, that's what we are trying to do something about."

Doubts bubbled up as the woman talked. Even Elvin had his eyes glued on Belinda while TJ was filming it. Possibly anxious for her aunt, Tawnee clenched her hands together. Didn't people normally hear the other side of the conversation in a séance? This wasn't a séance, just an ambush interview of sorts with a ghost. This was nonsense. It had to be. "What's he saying?"

Belinda blinked a few times as if she was unaware there were actually flesh and blood people in the room with her. "This is a house of sadness," she explained slowly. "There shouldn't be all these people marching through the house, disturbing the solitude."

"Why is he sad?" Nala assumed there'd be some standard answer such as he lost the only woman he ever loved.

"His daughter died here." She gave a heavy sigh. "I just feel darkness, heaviness." She pressed a hand to her chest. "Heartache."

She cocked her head as if she heard something else, she held up a hand, then dropped it. "He's gone."

Wait. This wasn't right. "How can he be gone? He lives here."

Belinda managed a weary shake of her head. "People tend to think that. Spirits can go wherever they want. I'm not even sure this house is his home, but he does visit it. It has something to do with his daughter."

That would make sense. Nala held her hands up in front of her and stared at them, then she slapped them together, attracting attention.

Elvin nudged her. "What are you doing?"

"Making sure this isn't a dream."

"A friend would help." He reached over and took a healthy portion of skin on her arm between his two fingers and twisted.

"Ouch! Why did you do that?"

"Just to prove you aren't dreaming." He smirked, then turned toward Belinda. "Did the spirit say anything about the missing girls?"

It wasn't a dream. It had to be a nightmare when spirits provided investigative advice or worse, living people thought they did.

"No." Her hands pushed through her hair. "I'm not a professional, not like on television. It isn't easy for me to walk in somewhere and start a conversation with the resident spirit. I need to be able to sit down, have my feet on the floor, and my hands resting on a table. What I need is…"

Nala closed her eyes and silently chanted *don't say it.*

"A séance."

She said it.

Chapter Ten

THE HARNESS AND leash hung loosely from Nala's fingers. According to the notes Regina left, Teddy liked going for walks. If it weren't for the mice building cities in the university office, Nala wouldn't even consider it. Everyone had their weakness. For Indiana Jones, it was snakes. Mice didn't merit the same fear as snakes do, but they chewed through your electrical cords, got into your cereal boxes, left mouse turds in your best Italian shoes, and sometimes at night, ran across your face. There would be no mice for her even if it took walking Teddy on a leash.

Max strolled into the room and took one look at the harness. "I'm not wearing that!"

"Of course, you're not. It's for Teddy."

"Good luck with that. It might be fun to watch. I don't want furzilla to think I was involved in any way."

"Coward. Elvin is coming by to pick you up, anyhow. After that bust at the haunted house, we now need to do some serious investigative work. We'll drop Teddy off at the office, lock him in mouse kingdom with a bowl of water, then come back in a couple of hours."

Max shot her a disbelieving look. "There's so much wrong with that plan."

Sometimes the easiest plans worked best. When had she turned into a person who took advice from her dog? She was at the top of the food chain, or was she? Pets had their human owners carting them around and going to work to afford their special food and daycare. There were even people who believed dogs were aliens who manipulated their human masters. Geesh. This case had her considering all sorts of crazy things besides just spirits. "Go ahead, tell me what's wrong with my plan."

"Glad you asked. I doubt Mr. Ted has caught a mouse in his life."

"Mr. Ted?"

"It's a compromise. I agree to call him Mr. Ted. He agreed not to rip off my face. It seemed fair." He managed a sheepish grin before continuing. "What if he messes the office up?"

The place was stuffed with books everywhere. What was there to mess up? It wasn't like it was a spread for some decorating maga-zine. "It's just piles of books."

"What if they're in order?"

That, she hadn't considered. It would make sense if Regina stacked books together on certain subjects, especially if she were doing research for her proposed book. Brownies! "You knocked down books."

"That's why I know it's so easy to do."

This caused a wrinkle in her plans. Surely, she could find an alternative. There were passive ways of getting rid of mice such as sticky traps, but that would mean she'd have to look into the tiny eyes of the rodent. Would she take it for a drive in the country and release it? Worse, that would mean touching it. *Yuck*. How far did you have to go to make sure it didn't return? Teddy was the only plan she had. "I'll take photos of the books. That way I can place them back in order."

"Ooo-kay." Max stretched out the word. A knock on the window made them both jump.

Elvin pressed his face against the window. "I'm here!"

In an effort not to look rattled by the sudden noise, she pushed her hair back behind her ear before heading for the door. Elvin entered the house rattling a white bakery bag. "I brought breakfast."

Whatever it was, it was guaranteed not to be healthy. As a man whose metabolism hadn't given up on him yet, he could eat anything and usually did, with no effect on his lanky frame. Max stuck his nose to the bag and wagged his tail. It couldn't be cheeseburgers.

"Thanks. What is it?"

"Donut holes. You did make coffee?"

"I did."

Regina had felt the need to warn her that the coffee at the university wasn't fit for consumption. A pot of coffee, already made, sat waiting to be poured into travel mugs.

"Explain our strategy again, mate."

Mate? Strategy? "Did you watch some Australian movie last night?"

"What if I did? I needed to de-escalate after our encounter with the spirit world."

Yeah, about that. She wasn't so certain, but she knew Elvin wanted to believe along with TJ. Belinda was Tawnee's aunt. She'd respect family bonds and say nothing. Still, there was no way she'd go to a séance. "You're not going to use that fake Australian accent all day, are you?"

"What's wrong with you, mate? Got something against the Aussies?"

"No, I do not have anything against the Aussies. I'm a big fan of Hugh Jackman."

"Ah, my girlfriend says the same thing." He rolled his eyes. "Women go crazy for men with an accent."

"Sometimes." She was thinking more of David with his posh British accent than the talented and handsome Australian actor.

"Don't understand it. I should go somewhere abroad. Then I'd have an accent, and the women would be all over me."

It would depend on if they could understand what he was saying. If they could, they might wonder if he was an alien with all his odd phrases taken from 1940s movies. "Yeah, you should try that some time. Anyhow, I was going to take Teddy to the office."

"Teddy? Are you using other consultants?" His brow furrowed, and his eyes widened.

She would have almost thought he was hurt, but Elvin could be just as dramatic as Max on occasions. There was a good chance her dog learned his various theatrics from observing Elvin. "Teddy is a cat. I need him to rid Regina's office of mice. I refuse to go back in there for office hours, which is a total waste of time. I know nothing about creative writing. Still…" She tapped one finger on her cheek. "That's where TJ and Tawnee found me to report the missing girl. I need an accessible location that possible sources can visit and relay information."

"That happens so much."

Actually, it didn't. "Not like on television. I'm still waiting for that reliable source to show up."

He placed the bag Max had been sniffing on the counter and reached for the harness in Nala's hands. "I used to have a cat. There's a trick to getting this on them."

"You had a cat?" She allowed him to take the harness to examine it.

"Yeah," he nodded and arched an eyebrow. "You say it like it's unbelievable. Samson. We named him that because he had long, flowing hair. That cat was amazing. Got him when I was eight, and I thought he would live forever. When he died, I decided not to get another pet, because it hurt so much when they were no longer around."

That surprised her. She never imagined Elvin as a cat fancier. Even though he liked Max, cat and dog people were not the same. She always imagined dog people as friendly, outgoing, and ready to play while cat people were reserved. They were watchers, not talkers, which didn't describe Elvin at all. This could be just another story to get her to feel sorry for him. Once she did, he'd laugh it off and tell her he just made it up. She'd see about that. "Okay, cat fan, go harness Teddy. He's in the living room."

Elvin shook the harness in his clutched fist. "I will. Make my coffee while I do. The way I like it, three sugars and lots of cream."

"Which is not coffee, but I will." She pointed to the direction of the living room just in case Elvin didn't know. He wouldn't ask. As her friend left the room, she filled the travel mugs, straining her ears for the sound of breaking glass. *Nothing.* Well, she *had* cleared the area of breakables. Whatever Teddy knocked over in the process wouldn't shatter. Still, she expected to hear something.

Just as soon as she finished fixing Elvin's coffee, the man entered the room carrying Teddy and cooing to the feline. "Who's the bad boy now?"

Bad boy sounded right. It made her wonder what had happened. "Any trouble?"

"None." Elvin regarded the cat with an adoring look. "Who's the gorgeous feline in the house?" As if he had doubts the cat would answer, he did. "It's Teddy."

"He prefers to be called Mr. Ted." Now she was quoting her dog. Fortunately, Elvin didn't ask how she knew this.

The cat lay unresisting in Elvin's arms, returning the look of adoration. *Weird.* Maybe her friend was the cat whisperer. "The two of you are getting along so well, you could bring him in your car. Max and Mr. Ted can't ride in the same car."

She expected an argument. Instead, Elvin looked up and agreed. "Sure. It must be hard for two alpha males to be in the same place."

How thoughtful and sweet Elvin was. The man needed a pet if it had this much of a softening effect on him.

"Besides," he added, "I'm surprised both you and Max can fit into that tin can you call a car. That time I rode in it, I was sure I'd have to call the fire department to use the jaws of life to release me."

The soft and fuzzy side was gone again. If Teddy had any effect, it was limited. Could be the cat's general bad mood could be catching. "It's good you brought your own vehicle, so you don't have to ride in my hipster tin can."

She opened the bakery bag, popped a donut hole in her mouth and threw one to Max, who had been waiting for such a happening and snatched it out of the air. They could pack on extra weight together. Max loved to eat but showed no side effects from doing so.

His metabolism must be on steroids.

"Your car is not a hipster vehicle."

Before Elvin could say more, she stuffed a donut hole into his open mouth.

"Sez you." She gathered up the mugs, shouldered her purse, and grabbed the bakery bag at the last minute. For a moment there, she almost sounded like her dog. There were plenty of articles with photos about people looking like their pets, but not a one about talking like them. Of course, Max imitated Elvin, who usually mimicked anyone he saw in the movies. She'd have to make an effort not to repeat anything that sounded like her dog. "It's time to hit the road."

TEDDY WALKED PROUDLY with his head held high, unlike the cats she usually saw on a leash, either pulling ahead or flat on their backs refusing to move. It showed Regina did walk him and probably even took him to the university. There was no issue taking him to the office. It was as if he knew the way. Students stopped them every now and then to ask what Teddy was. Most thought he was some exotic animal. It turned out that Teddy gathered more attention and comments than Max.

Even though Max disliked it, she leashed him while at the university. He growled when another student made a fuss over Teddy. "I know, buddy. College students can be so fickle."

They entered the office level, opened the door, and Teddy darted in with Elvin behind. She took off to get some water for the feline. When she came back Teddy was inspecting the room. Elvin glanced up at her entrance. "I unhooked the leash. Afraid it might get caught on something as he decimated the mice."

"Any luck?"

"No. I assume cats have a great sense of smell. What he's probably sniffing is the scent of his owner. Could be he thinks she's hiding behind a pile of books."

"You're probably right." She knelt to place the dish of water on the floor. "We shouldn't be gone too long."

Max showed a level of intelligence she hadn't expected, staying out in the hallway to wait. If there was some way to ratchet up a situation, her dog could. Teddy's head swiveled around as she closed the door after Elvin's exit. Most people would say he would be confused by her actions but he wasn't. His glare served as a promise that retribution would be taken. Now she was starting to sound like her dog. Once they got outside, Elvin pointed in the direction of the parking lot.

"Let's take my rental. Wyn has seen yours and besides, all my equipment is in mine. We know it won't fit into your metal mint box of a car."

"Ha. Ha." At least he called it a candy box, instead of a tin car. He was right, though. The equipment wouldn't fit into the beetle. She had no clue a trip to cover Regina's classes would end up chasing down missing girls, and she'd brought no evidence bags or parabolic microphones to eavesdrop on conversations. Nope. Just her, Max, and an assortment of professional outfits she usually reserved for meeting with clients. "Why the rental? What did you bring?"

The two of them strolled to the parking lot with occasional stops for students to pet Max, which caused him to pick up a little more energy. A happy dog would make it better for everyone.

"The babe magnet machine has no storage. I brought a finger-print kit, listening devices, high definition camera with zoom lens, and get this, I got some special items, too. You'll be excited."

She chuckled. "Remembering the last time and how excited I got over your spy gadget, I'm afraid to ask. The shoe knife, if you don't remember, or was it a shoe with a knife in it. Even better, an excuse to work on your Fandango moves."

"Forget about that. I have. This is so much better. I got a soda bottle that functions as a camera. You just walk down the street carrying the bottle in front of you and film as you go. Then there's a pair of thick frame glasses that looks like something from the 1950s. Still, you can film as you go."

True. "I'm not sure the glasses would work. The idea is not to attract attention and blend in, which would be hard with such fake glasses. As for the soda bottle, maybe. Still, I'm not sure why when I can walk around with my phone that has forward and back cameras. I can pretend to be texting and record or even act like I'm taking a selfie while filming a possible suspect. I already have a phone."

"You know how to suck the fun out of things." He grimaced. "At least I should be able to get some use out of them."

"Send them back." They had continued to walk as they talked. They made it to Elvin's rental, which was exactly the type of car not to merit a second look. "Was storage the only reason for the rental?"

"I figured if I was going to take a road trip, a rental would be better."

"Of course. I know you don't want anything to happen to your baby. It wasn't the possibility of your car being covered with dog hairs that did it?"

"Remember leather seats. It isn't an issue. No. Abby didn't want me zooming around and impressing any strange women."

It was tempting to say something—maybe a little zinger about how that had never happened in the past—but she settled instead for a kinder response. "Kind of you to ease her mind."

"I'm good like that." The fob beeped releasing the car doors. Nala held the back door open and Max vaulted into the back seat, scattering whatever was on it. Elvin groaned, but Nala chose to ignore it. When you live with a dog, you tried not to get excited about the little things. She scooted onto the passenger seat and waited for Elvin to get in and start the car.

"How should we play this?"

"Depends." The car engine came to life. "Has Wyn seen you?"

"Wyn probably saw me since he slipped out the back door when I arrived, without even knowing why I was there. Come to think of it, I don't even know what he looks like."

"That could be an issue." Elvin waggled his eyebrows at what he considered a witticism, then backed out.

"It's been crazy with Teddy and all. I need to know what he looks like."

"Yep. So, where are we going?" Elvin asked.

"2222 Linda Drive. It's his parents' house. If I go in again, they might expect a scholarship. Long story."

"We could follow Wyn if we knew what he looked like."

"We're back to that again." She held up her phone. "Do you have a hotspot with this car?"

"Not sure. Probably not. I just wanted something basic with cargo space."

"Here's an idea. If nothing else, we can go online. It will take time without a hotspot." She spoke into her phone, "Friendbook," then turned slightly to address Elvin. "Do you think he uses the name Wyn on his social media sites? I doubt it's his actual name."

"Probably still uses Wyn. No one uses their real name on social media."

"I use mine."

"Nala, move into this century. Even people who have social media sites in their own names, also have another one with a different name just for fun or something else."

This wasn't news to her, but she allowed Elvin to ramble on about a subject that was dear to him. Could Wyn have another social media site? Right now, she just needed to figure out what the guy looked like.

Chapter Eleven

THE TINY PHOTO on her phone showed a boy with out-of-control, dark hair. Nala scrolled down though Google images to look for another picture, bypassing all the tiny thumbnails displaying older men and a couple of women under the same name. Finally, she found a similar picture for Wyn Samuelson. Same face. Same hair. Right age. Using her fingers, she enlarged the photo to show a confident grin. A handsome male who probably thought he was entitled to whatever he wanted, including any female his interest might land on.

Something *had* happened with Ashlee. She knew it. The question was what. Among all the footprints, there was no blood. It would be hard to say if a struggle took place with most of the mansion trashed. With all the kids trespassing, it probably had been trashed for a while. Weird that there were still furnishings in the place. Most owners would have stored the furniture or sold it. Even more peculiar, a portrait falls off the wall at just the right time to heighten the suspense.

"Elvin, don't you think it's odd that there's furniture in the house?"

Her friend grunted as an acknowledgment but kept his eyes on the road ahead. After a lengthy interval, he replied with a disinterested mien. "Not sure what's so weird about furniture. Most people have it. Sure, Teddy is big, but I can't see him knocking over a couch."

"Not Regina's house. The abandoned Victorian."

He gave her a sideways glance. "I knew that."

Sure, he did. He was also paying attention. She'd give him a pass since she hadn't been clear. "When we entered the old house, I saw furniture. I didn't think about it until just now. Why would someone leave the place furnished?"

"You have a point," Elvin concluded as he floored it, barely making it through a yellow light. "I think the better question would be why is there furniture left in a college town?"

"Ugh. Did you even look at that stuff? It's probably a mouse hotel. Obviously, you've never strolled through any of the stores when it gets close to going back to school time. They have entire dorm room plans with coordinating accessories and cute furniture."

"But this furniture would be free." He slowed at the changing light, which gave him enough time to shoot her a disbelieving glance. "Nada. Nothing. Zilch."

Free occasionally could tempt her, but she found out on more than one occasion the strings that went with it negated the bargain. "There would be the cost of a truck you have to borrow or rent."

"A tank of gas and a six pack of beer would serve." Elvin gave a casual shrug as he answered.

"That would be about fifty dollars depending on how big a gas tank the truck had. You can't get the couch out by yourself. How would you get someone to help you?"

"Pizza. A large with everything." He smacked his lips.

Max did the same, flicking slobber in her direction. Her pup loved pizza, but she wasn't a fan. It tended to make *him* gassy. Small house and large, flatulent dog were never a good combination.

"That's probably another twenty dollars or more. You're up to seventy. You and your helper will probably be covered with chigger bites from wading through the tall grass. Then, there's the possibility of being caught trespassing, which is a class A misdemeanor in Indiana with a fine of $5000 dollars or a year in jail."

A sharp whistle filled the car. "You won that round. No wonder the furniture is still there. Makes me wonder why anyone bothers sneaking into the place if there is such a stiff fine."

"Yeah, me too." There wasn't any charm to the place. "There has to be a ton of places to drink on the campus and off. I imagine it's the danger. The thrill of pushing the envelope. It's probably about ghosts and things that go bump in the night. I'm not even sure if the teens even know there's a fine for trespassing. They probably expect to get their hands slapped or their parents called."

"Not to mention being charged with malicious mischief."

"Sure, the place is a wreck, but I doubt you could pin it on one person. Time and weather play a big part, I bet. I'm sure they never give it a second thought. No one has been charged with trespassing. You checked the records?"

Elvin murmured something and checked his mirror. "You know what type of car Wyn drives?"

"Really? You're asking me that when I didn't even know what he looked like."

Elvin used his thumb to point to the rearview mirror. "I saw a jeep pull out of the neighborhood. It had some age, lots of dents, and so many bumper stickers on the back window that it would be hard to see through them."

"You could see through them?" she asked, knowing Elvin liked to boast of supernatural abilities that he did not have.

"No. I did briefly see a male with enough dark hair glued in some wild disarray that could qualify him as a boy band member." Elvin pointed to the next entrance into the neighborhood, "That's our turn. It makes sense he could leave the neighborhood by the exit we skipped."

"You're right. It could have been him. Why are you turning here when he's now gone?"

Elvin coasted to a stop in front of a brick ranch home that had a glow-in-a-dark sign of a running child by the driveway. "I figured I might as well stop by the wild child crossing until you decide which way we should go."

"Well, we don't know if that was Wyn. We can go by his house and see how many cars are there." It was not investigative work at its best. "In the meantime, I'll look on Friendbook to see if he posted a picture of his car. I heard males tend to treasure their wheels more than their girlfriends."

The car maneuvered through the rabbit-warren neighborhood with occasional stops for children dashing into the street. One was chasing a ball, the other a puppy. As they drew closer to the house, Elvin slowed. "If I go any slower, someone might offer to push my car out of the street."

"Just a minute. Wyn has taken more selfies of himself than you have. I'd understand dudes posting pictures of other dudes doing stupid things, hot girls, or even objects that look like something else, but it's Wyn grinning, winking, looking sultry with his eyes closed, etc. Here's something different. A shot of a rocket. His mother had mentioned he was into rocketry, but I thought that was just a lame excuse for when he took off. You know, like going to the library."

"I never said that. My parents wouldn't believe me."

Nala continued scrolling in hopes of finding a vehicle of any kind. "What did *you* say?"

"I was going to Radio Shack."

Only Elvin would use such an excuse. "Where did you go?"

"Radio Shack."

"No."

"Yes. They had wires, connectors, batteries. Everything I needed for my little projects. I even got my first stereo kit there."

For a moment there, she forgot who she was talking to. They slid slowly past 2222 Linda. There were no cars in front of the ranch or in the driveway. There could be cars hidden in the garage, but her previous visit established Wyn's mother was a collector. There had been shelves for crystal bells and a curio cabinet filled with some type of ugly dolls and an unwieldy stack of magazines in the corner of the living room. Collectors usually didn't have clean garages that could shield a car from the rain. Usually, everything they moved to make room for their collections went into the garage, attic, or spare bedroom. The drawn curtains could mean no one was home or whoever was, wanted privacy.

"Not feeling it. How about you?"

Elvin pulled up in front of the next house and parked. "Give me the phone. You're taking forever. I bet you're reading the captions."

"What if I am?" She pressed the phone to her chest with one hand. "They could be very revealing."

"Have they been?"

"Not really." She grimaced as she surrendered the phone. "I did find out he really does have a real-life interest in rocketry. That's something. Maybe he does hang out at the hobby shop. How many of those can there be in town?"

"Depends on nerds per mile," Elvin smirked as he scrolled, then stopped. "Got it." He flashed an image of a beaming Wyn beside the jeep. "It's the one I saw. It *was* him."

"Where could he be going?"

"Almost anywhere." Elvin handed back the phone and covered his head with one hand and groaned. "How do you do this?"

"Focus on what you know, not what you don't know. Why don't you let me drive for a while? I know this area better than you."

"Ha! You just want to know what it feels like to have a vehicle actually move when you stomp on the gas."

He opened his door as a sign of agreement. Knowing he might change his mind, Nala pocketed her phone, swung her own door wide and slid out. They passed each other at the back of the car and slapped hands.

Totally inconspicuous, not really, but at least they'd be gone in a couple of seconds and they did use a different car. There was the sound of a dog barking as something streaked past her. Could it have been a cat? Maybe a weasel? It was hard to say what it was. A pair of dogs charged after it in full pursuit. Fig bars! "Close the doors!"

She lurched for hers and got it slammed in time. Instead of eliminating the exit, Elvin called across the car hood. "What did you say?" At the same time, Max jumped out of the car in pursuit of the running dogs and whatever they might be chasing.

Nala sighed and leaned against the car. "I said close the door. Max is prone to run after animals in motion, even other dogs. It's a canine thing."

"Now you tell me." Elvin sprinted after the fast disappearing shepherd.

Nala puffed out a breath of air that ruffled her bangs as she debated if she should wait inside the car or out. She settled against the car. If her friend would have waited and didn't feel like he had to do everything in a typical alpha fashion, she would have told him Max always came back. Sometimes it took a while, but usually not too long. Unfortunately, Wyn would be moving, and she had no clue where. There was his house, which he was not at. He could hit the hobby store. How often did those involved in hobbies visit a shop? Her shoulders went up in a shrug. It was a subject she had no knowledge on. She assumed everyone ordered their supplies online.

It was a weekday, so it was possible Wyn had returned to school. All she needed was his class schedule, which wouldn't be too hard to get if she could check into the school computers with Regina's password, which she didn't have. Of course, there was no reason for her to have it. She wouldn't be inputting any grades. That avenue led to nothing. Where else might the difficult to catch male slip off to?

Would he return to the haunted mansion? There was the saying about criminals returning to the scene of their crime. Personally, she always thought it was an idiotic thing to do. Could be that Wyn wasn't the sharpest knife in the drawer. Still, it did not answer what happened to Ashlee or the other girls. Tawnee might be more help on that.

A rustle in the nearby shrubbery announced Max poking his

head out. Winded, his pale tongue lolled out as he wiggled out the rest of his body. He trotted over to the car, glanced at the back door and gave her an expectant look.

She knew the drill and opened the door, which allowed Max to jump in the back seat and lie down. "Boy, I needed a good run. That was fun."

"What were you chasing?"

"Who knows? It's all about the chase, not what spurred the run."

"I'll keep that in mind the next time we happen to be the object of the chase."

Bark! Bark! Bark!

The dog had gone back to his first language, which he often did when associating with other canines. Nala glanced at her watch. Ten minutes had gone by since Max's impulsive run and still no Elvin. A neighbor came out and pointedly stared at her. She waved. Often friendliness eliminated suspicion. It really shouldn't if people realized how many con artists depended on that fact.

"I'm waiting on my boyfriend who went to go look for our dog."

The woman pointed to the SUV Nala was leaning on. "Do you have two dogs?"

Ah yes, someone with good eyesight and the ability to see the obvious. It paid to stay as close to the truth as possible, especially if she bumped into the same people again. "Max came back right away. My boyfriend is probably lost in that bit of woods back there."

The woman turned toward the trees in question. "There's not much there. If he got lost, there's no one to ask for directions."

"Ha! Ha!" She forced a laugh and warmed up to her role. "That sounds like my sweetie. Even if there was someone to give directions, he'd never ask. My sugar dumpling would rather wander in circles forever."

"Untrue. Your dumpling is back." A disheveled Elvin came around the bush and straightened his glasses. He did a double take when he noticed Max in the car and pointed to him.

Understanding the unspoken question, she answered. "He came back in about five minutes. I would have told you he would, but you took off after him before I could."

The curious neighbor gave a wave. "It's nice to see people in love. Sometimes I think people forget what it feels like to be in love. Glad you found everyone."

"Me, too," Nala answered and opened the driver car door, assuming the conversation was over.

Apparently, the neighbor didn't feel likewise. She cupped her hands around her mouth and yelled. "Who were you coming by to see?"

This was awkward. There'd be no reason for them cruising through a random neighborhood, then losing their dog. Neighbors usually knew the best gossip. Besides, what could the neighbor say except a couple with a dog came by, which could be anyone. She made it a point not to mention Elvin's name in the conversation. "We came by to see the Samuelsons, but they aren't home." She decided to use Wyn's last name in the conversation.

Miss Curious used her hand to shade her eyes to peer over in her neighbor's direction and stated the obvious. "Nope. They aren't home."

Thank goodness. It would be embarrassing if they *were* home. The helpful neighbor would probably trot over there and knock.

"Both Art and Helen work. They're usually at church on Friday and Saturday. It's not *church* church, but a temple or something. Still, they're decent neighbors. No problems. Rachel, their daughter, married about a year ago. Winston, the son, is going to school and works at that teen shop in the mall. Hot something—I can't remember the last part of it. I never go to it because it's dark, and they play that awful music. Come back tonight and they should be home."

"Thanks."

"Whom should I say came by?"

Before she could answer Elvin did, "Elvis and Priscilla."

The neighbor laughed and fanned herself with her hand. "He's a keeper."

Elvin grinned and addressed Nala as he slid into the passenger side. "I'm a keeper."

"I heard." She started the car. "Where to?"

"Hobby shop."

"Look it up then."

She smiled and waved at the woman and checked to make sure their windows were closed. As the motored away, she felt some sympathy for the nosy neighbor. "Did you hear her say it was nice to see people in love? It sounds like there isn't much love in her life."

"I was caught in the shock of you calling me sugar dumpling. Is there something I need to relay to my girlfriend?"

"Please." She wrinkled her nose. "It was acting."

"I know. Not the best either, but hopefully good enough for the neighbor. Could be she's suspected her neighbors of being spies or aliens forever and our visit just gives her more fodder."

They maneuvered around the streets as Nala searched for an

opening. "Got anything on a hobby store address?"

"Nag. Nag. Nag. I remember when our love was new."

"Address?"

Elvin tapped on his phone before replying. "There's nothing here in New Albany. The closest place is Clarksville." He made a few more taps and muttered "Aha!"

"Aha, what?"

"There's a Hot Something store in Clarksville."

Nala shook her head in disbelief. "You're kidding me. That's the name of an actual store?"

Elvin replied "Yep. We're bound to find him in one of those places."

"Maybe. Did you get the list of missing girls for me?"

"I did."

"Notice anything odd about it?"

"Depends."

Why did the man tease her like this? She glanced back into her mirror to make sure no one was following her and stomped on the brake. Remembering her dog in the back at the last minute, she apologized. "Sorry, Max. Not sorry, Elvin."

"What was that about?"

"Just say what you have to say without being cute about it."

"Says the woman who is PMSing."

She jabbed her friend in the side, using a stiff finger. The sound of a car coming up behind her set her back into motion. "That's so rude! It's typical, too. Whenever you guys can't accept women have a right to be angry, frustrated, or upset, you blame it on the menstrual cycle." A glance in the rear view mirror revealed the car was following her closer than she'd like. Not surprising, since they were going slower than they should. A tap to the gas got them moving.

"Hey, I'm not the person you're mad at."

Mad might be overstating the case. "We have very limited time here. You came to help. So, help."

"I'm really here to help."

"Yes, you are. Care to share the address?"

Elvin stayed silent as he punched in the GPS address.

A modulated female voice spoke with a tinge of a British accent. "Turn left on Green Valley."

Which she did. GPS was great when it worked and didn't take her the wrong way or failed to work due to heavy cloud cover. That was true of everything. It was great when it worked. Hopefully, with a little help from Elvin and Max, they could all work together and bring Ashlee back home. That is, if she wanted to come back home.

Chapter Twelve

THE TALL SIGN for the mall towered over all the shorter stores and restaurants. Nala steered toward it since it was easier to see. Wyn heading to work or school made more sense than going to a hobby shop. The only problem with the mall was Max. "Do you think I can bring Max into the mall?"

"Sure. Everyone loves Max."

Sometimes it was almost impossible to get a serious answer from her friend and sometime work associate. "I don't want to get chased out. Still, I see a lot of folks walking around stores with their dogs."

"Uh-huh. Would those stores feature concrete floors and outdoor furniture for sale?"

"Some do."

"I think a store that isn't too fancy will let you bring a dog in. Others that sell clothes or food probably have an agreement with the department of health not to have live animals inside. Those little tiny boutique stores you women like so much that squeeze too much stuff in every inch of the place are an accident waiting to happen when it comes to Max."

Bark! Bark!

"See, you upset Max. All right, I'll go in, and you stay in the car with Max."

She parked the car, grabbed her purse, and swung open the door, not sure what she'd say to Wyn when she met him. It would come to her as she walked. It usually did. Most people might hold to a standard inquiry form, but she felt different situations called for different approaches. Did you kill Ashlee would *not* be the best one. That much she did know.

Before she even closed the car door, Elvin called after her. "The two of us will need to wait on you so bring us a treat."

Bark! Bark! Max seconded the request.

"I'll see what I can do." She weaved in between the cars at a race walk, sometimes bumping against trucks with protruding hitches, bruising her shins in the process. When she tried to keep her eyes out for shin-beating hitches, she bumped into an extended side view mirror. Sugar Cookies! This place was a hazard zone. The nearby glass entry doors beckoned her with promising sanctuary and a possible lemon shake-up.

When she reached the door, she reminded herself to breathe in, hold it, then breathe out to relax. Only the mall walkers rushed around this place. Everyone else strolled as if they had all the time in the world, which she totally didn't. Every minute counted in finding a missing person. Any assistance would be welcomed. Ashlee's mother was next on her list. Maybe she should have been the first. After all, the woman got an Amber Alert out, so she took her daughter's disappearance seriously.

A kiosk with the store names on it informed her the store she needed was in the West Wing. Why did they label things that way? Someone, possibly the architect, assumed everyone could tell cardinal directions inside a building without the help of the sun, or they assumed they had a compass with them. The map displayed where she was as a red dot. If she walked toward Penney's, she should be close. She started walking, wondering how she would approach her suspect. The professional approach usually rattled. Just the mention of being a licensed private investigator confused most. They wrongly assumed she was somehow connected to the police. Those who didn't, thought she was some no-holds-barred bounty hunter who would hog-tie them and throw them into the car trunk. If Max was with her, they especially thought the latter.

Mall traffic was light with a few mothers pushing strollers with unhappy toddlers. There was a handful of people strolling around with nametags who she assumed were mall employees, either going to work or coming back from a break. A few employees loitered near the front of their stores smiling at her until she passed by them. Abrasive, overloud music assaulted her ears. She winced. Someone needed to turn that off. She searched for the source and if she found a handy extension cord, she'd be tempted to pull it. Even though there were four stores nearby, she noticed the mothers with strollers cut to the other side of the walkway to avoid one store. Even two mall walkers stopped as if hitting a wall, then changed direction. She wished she had sent Elvin in, but as good as her friend was at finding things via computers, he wasn't that good in person.

He'd talk plenty and would sometimes get the other person into discussions about which sports team would win or what motorcycle was best, never anything she needed to solve her case. That's why she came in today. That's also why she'd steel herself to go into the noisy place with the T-shirts on display that featured rude messages. This was exactly the type of place her mother would refuse to allow her to visit when she was younger, which made it even more of a treat for her and her best friend, Karly, to sneak into. They never bought anything. There was never anything they wanted. No, all they wanted was to say they had been there to their friends. She even took a selfie to prove it, which her mother somehow found out about. Gwen Bonne, her mother, had more sources than the FBI, especially when it came to the mall.

The store wasn't crowded, and she assumed most of its clientele was at school. A male clerk leaned next to the cash register texting. He never even looked up as she entered or greeted her. It wouldn't be too hard to shoplift in the place. A round display held jackets loaded with logos. Nala pushed them around and turned over a price tag. She blinked. Surely, she read the numbers wrong. Shouldn't there be a decimal in there somewhere?

"Can I help you?" A smiling woman with a magnetic name tag stuck to her T-shirt gestured to the jackets. "I can unlock one, so you can try it on."

"They're locked?" She hadn't noticed. At that price, she could well understand why. She pointed to a jacket that was approximately her size and waited for the woman to unlock it. A person in hopes of making a sale, especially a pricey one, would be forthcoming. She hoped.

"Yes. It's a hassle, but you'd be surprised how many things walk off when they're not locked down." She unlocked the jacket and handed it to Nala. "I'm Desiree, the day manager. Let me know if there's anything I can do for you."

As manager, she should know plenty about Wyn and when he worked. She tried on the garish jacket that fit fairly well. Desiree must have noticed the fit, too. "Woo, that looks good on you."

It would be fun to show up at the usual Sunday lunch with her parents and watch her stylish mother squirm trying to figure out if the jacket was a serious purchase or a practical joke without coming right out and asking. "Ah, thanks. I was kinda hoping Wyn was working today."

"Not today. Is he your nephew or something?"

Naturally, Desiree assumed she was an older relative as opposed to a contemporary cousin or even a friend. "Cousins twice re-moved." That should make it distant enough for Wyn to not know her.

"Oh, I understand." Desiree shook her head. "He doesn't work until Friday. Business has been slow, and I haven't been able to give him much work. I guess you were hoping for the family discount."

It made a good excuse for her appearance, although she couldn't corner him inside the store with Desiree working. "You caught me. If he isn't here, I might as well go."

The manager's forehead furrowed as she put a fist to her mouth. Nala slid off the jacket, but before she could put it back on the locking hanger, Desiree stopped her. "Wait. I'll give you the family discount if you agree to wear the jacket and tell everyone where you got it."

Her eyebrows shot up.

"I know it's crazy, but I think it might help seeing someone of your age wearing the jacket. It might bring in a different demo-graphic."

It sounded like she had been called *old* in an offhand fashion. Worse, she'd have to buy the jacket to not blow her cover. Snicker-doodles! This trip was costing her money, instead of making her money. She needed some disability and insurance jobs where she could sit at a desk all day and scroll through people's social media files to see how sick they really were.

Ten minutes later, she was standing in line wearing a bold jacket that practically screamed *look at me* waiting to get hot pretzels for Elvin and Max. She decided to forgo the dipping cheese for the both of them. When she got to the car, Max accepted his pretzel with grace. Elvin not so much.

"Where's my hot cheese?"

"They were out."

"Why are you wearing that awful jacket? Wait. Don't tell me you're on one of those secret camera shows." He rolled down his window to stick out his head as if he could catch a glimpse of a cameraman.

"I don't want to talk about it." She slid into the front seat and started the car. "No Wyn. It was a bust."

"Surely not. You got that snazzy new jacket. I'm sure that's what all the cool kids are wearing," Elvin teased, smiling, and went so far as to wink.

Oh, he was enjoying it. "Shut up and give me the directions to the hobby shop."

"Sure, whatever you say. Um, what should I call you in that outfit? Superstar? Killer Queen? Boss?"

"Very funny. Boss will do."

"Got it. We're close. Go out the exit by the liquor store and turn right. I get to go in this time."

She maneuvered through the slow-moving walkers headed to their cars, then had to wait at the light. Elvin had his fun at her expense. No surprise. "I think you would be perfect for the hobby shop. You have that right amount of dweeb factor. It's easy to see you putting together model airplanes while alone in your bedroom."

"Correction. I was making electronic components, which made me the helpful citizen I am. If I hadn't done that, I wouldn't be what I am today."

"I'll give you that." She slowed for the next red light. "Do I turn here?"

"Yeah, left."

"It would have been nice to know that before I got in the right lane. Now I have to work my way across three lanes of traffic."

"My bad."

The sound of a window powering down had Nala glancing into the mirror. Max stuck out his head and barked. Bark! Bark! Bark!

"What's your dog doing?"

"I believe he's trying to help me get across the lanes. Several people pointed at Max and commented as Nala turned on the signal. Surprisingly, she got across the lanes and was able to turn. Near a fast food restaurant was an unremarkable strip mall filled with small stores and wood signs announcing the businesses. One announced a hobby shop. In front of it were a few parked vehicles, including the jeep.

"Bingo!"

Elvin slapped the dashboard. "Pay dirt. I need you to use the parabolic mike and record. It's in the back. We just have to make it look like we're doing something ordinary and not weird."

"I bet you brought the really big one, too, as opposed to the smaller one that looks like something from an old sci-fi flick."

"You're half-right. I brought both."

They decided to park the car not facing the hobby shop so as to not look too suspicious. They had the parabolic mics set up, and then Elvin straightened and ran his hands through his hair, messing his carefully created style. It was totally out of character for the man.

"What are you doing?"

"I can't be too styling, or someone might consider it odd I'm heading into a hobby store."

"Just say it's a gift for your nephew."

"Good one." He gave her a thumbs up and sauntered to the store door. He had an additional mic on his body, too.

Nala leaned over the mic and tried to bring in the surrounding sounds. Their decision to park not facing the shop brought in road sounds and two girls on lunch break in a nearby car, gossiping about a third girl who was not there. Not helpful. The earbud in her headset came to life.

"I'm in and looking at WWII aircraft. Here comes somebody."

"Hello. Can I help you?" said an unknown voice.

"Sure. I'm looking for a present for my nephew."

There was the sound of two guys talking in the background. She was getting every other word. "Trouble…Ashlee…Scared."

It sounded like her boy, but she needed more and better reception. "Looks like we're moving the car, Max."

"Not sure why I couldn't go in. No one suspects dogs are listening."

"True." She started the engine and slowly moved in closer, trying to listen as she did so. Elvin kept turning down various offers of various models, despite the man finding the exact models he asked for. He probably made the mistake of assuming the man didn't have any of the hard to find models he suggested. He just found someone who was possibly geekier than he was. As they got closer, she heard who she assumed was Wyn. "I needed the money. Cheese isn't free. I ran through the prescription meds I lifted from my grandparents and couldn't get any more hours at the mall."

"Still, it's peculiar. Sounds like something from one of those spy movies. How did you hear about it?"

"Jack told me. It's a game he played with his girlfriend. It's kinda like those escape rooms. The difference is just the woman has to escape."

"It sounds wack. You got paid for this?"

"Not yet. Jack's holding out on me. What a liar!"

"What did he say?"

Nala leaned closer to the dish of the parabolic as if that would help her hear better. Elvin's voice sounded over whatever was being said between the young men. "Yes, I think my nephew might be interested in a rocket."

Something weird was up, especially if someone was paying for women to be lured to the house. It didn't sound like ghosts to her. Just when Wyn was going to spill details, Elvin cut off the conversation. What she'd heard didn't mean they shouldn't talk to Wyn, especially now that they had something to discuss.

When Wyn came out of the store, Nala ducked down. If he was in a hurry, he would assume the parabolic mic was a satellite dish that was being returned. Then again, her father pointed out that most people don't notice stuff, too caught up in their own world. That was why eyewitnesses weren't really that good while circumstantial evidence could be more dependable.

Another car door slammed, which she assumed was the friend, then the door on her side opened. Elvin had three boxes tucked under his arm as he asked, "What are you doing?"

"Not attracting attention when Wyn came out."

"I kinda got that. The hunched down position gave it away."

She straightened, then slid out of the car as they moved all the equipment except the tape recorder. "There's some weird stuff going on here. Listen to the tape. As much as I want to solve this case, I think we need to bring in the police."

Chapter Thirteen

T HE STRIP MALLS and convenience stores all blended into one another as they left Clarksville and headed back to New Albany. Elvin had in earplugs and was listening to the store recording while Max rested his chin on her shoulder and whispered in her ear.

"Cheeseburger. I could smell it. So close. I got nothing. I've spent the entire morning inside the car except for a brief pit stop. You owe me."

It was unfair to park by a fast food restaurant and not get him anything. If she knew one thing about her dog, he could be relentless when it came to his favorite food. Even though she tried to feed him a healthy diet of the balanced, organic dog food the veterinarian suggested, he wasn't accepting of it, unless there was nothing else. Instead, he'd nag and nag until she broke. If she were a parent she'd probably be the indulgent one all the other mothers heard about via their children. Litanies like *Max's mother lets him have cheeseburgers for breakfast* and so on.

"Okay! I'll get you a cheeseburger."

Elvin removed his earbuds and gazed at her in surprise. "You must be psychic. I was feeling a bit peckish. A cheeseburger or two would do me. With fries. No reason going to a drive-thru if you don't get fries."

"We'll do that on our way to see Ashlee's mother. I should have gone there first. She is the one most motivated to find her. I went with Wyn because he was the last one to see her."

"Don't second guess yourself. Either way would make sense. I think we have enough on Wyn to make him a person of interest. Do you think the police questioned him?"

"I have no clue." She shrugged. "Tawnee told me Ashlee was a super overachiever. I doubt she'd tell her parents she was going out with some bad boy to do some trespassing and who knows what else."

"Good point." Elvin pointed to his right. "There's a burger place ahead."

"I see it. I'm turning." She heard an audible sigh behind her. At least she was making the passengers happy.

After a quick food stop, they headed to Ashlee's neighborhood. Normally, she didn't do missing people and wasn't sure how to approach the parents. "I think we should take Max with us. Everyone loves dogs."

"Except for the people who don't like them."

"That number is so small, it would practically be minuscule. I'm sure they're dog fans. If not, they will appreciate him in his official capacity." She gave a small *humph* deciding the matter was settled.

A pair of lions topped off columns at the entrance of the neighborhood, a grandiose touch rather like an English manor house. She assumed those who lived here paid for the privilege to engage in such behavior. A landscape service cut trees and vacuumed up fallen leaves. Colorful mums provided splashes of color against the green expansive lawns. Pumpkins and corn shuck bundles decorated several porches. One had a scarecrow casually sitting on wrought iron furniture. Another had a skeleton as a nod to the approaching holiday. A few high-end cars were in the drive, but most were hidden behind the multi-car garage doors.

"Looks like Ashlee has a pretty posh life."

"Possibly. I could pull up her parents' financial records and see how solid they really are."

"No need." She had a personal policy of only nibbing when the job required it. However, she might benefit from researching her dates ahead of time. "Here it is." She pulled into a curved driveway in front of an Italianate mini-mansion.

"This isn't looking like dog people to me. If they have one, it's only an accessory that fits into a purse."

Even though she thought the same, she often liked to needle her friend. "Being a tad judgmental, aren't you?"

The sound of a dog barking alerted them their arrival had been noticed. A slender woman in an expensive pants suit stepped out on the porch and in doing so released a large dog of indiscriminate heritage. Max pushed up against the window and erupted into a frenzy of barking.

"Stop!" Nala parked the car and turned off the ignition. Maybe she wouldn't bring Max with her. She powered the window down. "Hello, Mrs. Bolen."

The woman slowly picked her way to the car and clapped her hands together, calling back the dog. "You're not an annoying reporter, are you?"

"Oh, no, ma'am. I'm a personal investigator. You daughter's friend, Tawnee, asked me to look into her disappearance."

A tear welled up in one eye. "At least you acknowledge that much. I've had others suggest she ran away."

"Many teenagers do, which is why it's a common conclusion. Obviously, Tawnee doesn't. That's why she contacted me. I expect Ashlee would tell her friend more than her parents."

"Parent," the woman corrected. "I'm her mother, Noreen van Arsdale. I remarried years ago, but I would have to say, Ashlee never accepted her stepfather. My husband, Leon, can be a bit stern. He never had children of his own. I think that's why the police think she took off. Even though she's a good girl and never gave me a second's worry, Ashlee never made a secret of how she felt about Leon. She called him The Dictator."

"We heard," Nala acknowledged with a nod.

"The police think she'll be back when she's proven her point. I hope so, but I also think they are just blowing smoke because they're clueless."

Nala swung the door open. "Could we go inside and talk about this? I'm sure you don't want to share your business with your neighbors."

"Absolutely." Noreen glanced to either side of her. The neighbors' doors remained closed, but there was a twitch of the curtains at the house to the left. "Come in, bring your dog, too. Chance doesn't get many visitors."

Excellent. It would give Max an opportunity to converse with the dog. She wasn't sure how he did it, but he usually could tell what the other animals were thinking. Then, there was always *dog speak.* Her dog had informed her it didn't consist so much of actual words, but more feelings and intentions. Such as *Back up now or I'll tear your face off*, which could easily be read as fear. Fearful dogs were the most likely to attack.

"Okay, we're coming."

The three of them piled out of the car, and Noreen escorted them as the family dog brought up the rear. Inside, Noreen guided them to a large all-white living room complete with a white baby grand piano. "I'll get the dogs a little snack and get us some iced tea."

The clatter of dog nails meant Max had no issue following the woman. He usually didn't have issues when it came to treats. It made her wonder if Max would willingly frolic outside. Time would tell. She strolled around the spotless living room filled with oversized couches and lounges. Heavy, white, brocade drapes framed the window.

She muttered to Elvin, "I feel like I'm in one of those magazine spreads. I'm afraid to sit. I might dirty something."

"Maybe we could ask to go wherever the peons are allowed?"

"You may be a peon, but I'm a professional."

Noreen returned carrying a tray with a pitcher of iced tea and glasses. "I'm certainly glad you *are*, too. I've been getting nowhere with anyone. My husband thinks Ashlee is having a tantrum. I don't. Apparently, her friend doesn't, either."

"I agree." Nala stood, having basic etiquette drilled into her by her mother. She knew enough not to sit until her hostess did.

Noreen gestured to the plump couches. "Please sit and I'll pour you some tea." She did so and handed out the glasses, saying, "Tell me what you know."

This wasn't part of the plan. Nala came *for* information, not to give it out. Time to turn the tables. "Where did your daughter say she was going?"

"Ashlee said something about studying. I knew better. She spent a little extra time on her makeup and was wearing a new top. I suspected there was a boy involved. I didn't think it was a date, especially considering she had just broken up with her boyfriend, Cody."

"Do you mind if I take notes?" She retrieved her pen and pad. She flipped through her notes to see what Tawnee had said.

"Please do." The woman pressed her open hand against her chest. "I was curious, and I wanted to know. Things have been tense around here lately. I wanted my daughter to confide in me. Cornering her and demanding answers was not the scenario I wanted. Too bad I didn't see that right away. At first, I thought her father was involved. That's why I put the Amber Alert out."

Amber Alerts were usually issued by the police for missing babies and small children who would be easy enough to pick up and take off with. They'd also be clueless on how to protect themselves and easily lured with the use of a puppy or candy.

"It would be unusual for a non-custodial parent to take a teenager. They're able to resist and call for help. They also don't stay where they are put."

Their hostess pressed her fingers on the bridge of her nose. "Good points. I don't think Trevor would abduct our daughter. He can be charming and charismatic. Most people like him until they spend extended time with him. It wouldn't be beyond him to try to convince Ashlee to live with him. All he'd have to do is promise to loosen the apron strings."

"Would that appeal to your daughter?" Most teens would love having a mellow parent who let them do whatever they wanted.

"It might have in the past. Leon was worried about Ashlee getting too serious with her boyfriend. When they broke up, Ashlee confided that maybe Leon was right. With college just starting, it wasn't a good time to be in a relationship, especially since Cody was still in high school. Don't get me wrong. He's a good boy."

"You think Trevor wouldn't be able to seduce her to the dark side?" Elvin interjected.

Noreen's forehead puckered as she considered the remark. "He lives in Ohio. I'm not sure that would be considered the dark side. I wouldn't put it past him, though. Years ago, when Trevor left me, he was a bit of a rolling stone. I divorced him in absentia. A few years later, I met Leon." She gestured to the furnishings. "As you can see, he's been very generous to me."

And to himself, Nala added silently. "How does this impact Trevor?"

"Suddenly, he decided he wanted a relationship with our daughter. Never mind he never bothered to pay child support. To be fair, the court system couldn't find him. Trevor must have decided that life was passing him by and made contact. We arranged to meet in a public place. Leon drove us there. It went okay, considering Ashlee hadn't seen him for years. As soon as my daughter wasn't near, he started in on me claiming I had landed on my feet like a cat and some other things that weren't particularly nice."

"Jealous." Nala nodded her head. The behavior she described was the usually the way with a narcissist. They never liked the spotlight on anyone else. "Do you think he'd try to take your daughter to spite you?"

"It sounds extreme. My daughter wasn't acting secretive, packing bags, or fussing over her dog as if she wouldn't see him again. That's why I don't think she went to him. Besides, Ashlee knows how I worry. She'd have called me or at least texted me. Nothing."

It didn't bode well. Even runaways sometimes called to let their family know they were alive. "Peculiar. She sounds like an outstanding young woman. I'm sure you're very proud of her. We're going to do whatever we need to do to find her and return her back to you."

"Yes, please." The mother reached for Nala's hands and squeezed them. "I would be so grateful. I would pay you."

She was about to explain they'd taken the case free of charge when Elvin nudged her foot. Money would always help. "Let me tell you the story I received from Tawnee. Your daughter was going out with a new boy, not so much because she liked him, but to make the old boyfriend jealous."

"Who was he? Have the police questioned him?"

"I doubt the police have, because it appears they have no clue Ashlee was with him or that they decided to check out a local haunted house."

"Not that place." She pressed both hands to her cheeks. "Nothing good comes from there. I remember as a teen we used to sneak over there. I may even have mentioned this to her. It may be my fault."

"It's definitely not your fault, and I'm going to the police to see if I can interest them in the situation."

"Do your best. Now, about the boy."

It didn't take watching the movie of the week to know a parent would drive up to the house of the last person seen with their child and physically assault the person in question, mainly as a reaction to their ability to do nothing. No, it wouldn't help to mention the boy's name. Nala sucked in her lips trying to decide how she'd frame her refusal.

"Wyn Samuelson." Elvin cheerfully volunteered the information as if he was calling out bingo numbers.

Ginger Snaps! What had he done? Nala twisted her body to glare at her friend, who acted unaware of the possible consequences. In a television show, Noreen would explode in a rage, then run to get her loaded gun before tearing out of the place. In fiction, they always conveniently knew where the person they were seeking lived. Ashlee's mother remained seated with a perplexed expression and shook her head.

"Oh, no, no. Ashlee would have no interest in him. He's bad news. When she told me, he was attending her same college, I was shocked he'd even gotten in. No way she'd be interested in him. It makes no sense. There has to be something else—anything else."

Mothers saw what they wanted to see. Nala's own mother denied the attraction her own bad boy had exerted on her. However, her policeman father hadn't and followed them, confronted her date, and ended up taking Nala home in the squad car. She doubted Leon had anything on her father.

Still, it would be best to be cautious due to Elvin letting the pro-verbial cat out of the bag. "Wyn is handsome, which would be good if she was really trying to get Cody back. Guys are weird like that. They always want what someone else has."

"I just don't know." Noreen paced the floor while wringing her hands. Even distressed, she still managed to be classically beautiful with her smooth bob hairstyle, wide-spaced eyes, and understated makeup, all of which meant Ashlee was possibly a looker, too.

"Should I talk to Wyn's parents?"

Elvin and Nala answered together. "No!"

If somehow Noreen hadn't got the message, Nala shook her head several times. "Please don't. I know you mean well, but they could view it as an attack, even if you used words as opposed to fists, which I know you'd never do."

"When it comes to my daughter, I might do a lot of things that might surprise you."

The sound of a door closing and footsteps coming their way interrupted. "Noreen, who's car is that in the driveway?" A tall, balding man with ramrod posture entered the living room and regarded both Nala and Elvin with mistrust and wrapped one arm around his wife's shoulders.

Nala felt like an oily spot on the white couch—one he wanted removed immediately. She stood and held out her hand. "I'm Nala Bonne, private investigator. This is my associate Elvin Snopes. We were retained by your stepdaughter's friend, Tawnee, to look into her disappearance."

He dropped his arm from his wife's shoulder, took her hand, and gave it a firm shake. "Leon van Arsdale. Ashlee's stepfather. Tawnee?" His voice swung up in surprise on the name. "She has no money. Tell me who you really are. You're some of those no-good reporters who call themselves journalists as if that gives you the right to pry into people's personal life."

His eyes narrowed as he glared at them, and his stance shouted former military or possibly law enforcement. His rigid posture reminded her of her father and his views on young romance. It was no wonder her dating life had been slim to none when she lived at home. Her father had frightened every boy who asked her out. Leon probably did likewise. That meant Cody must love Ashlee very much. Mental note. Talk to Cody. Right now, she'd have to deal with the insult to her professionalism.

"I'm not a reporter." She reached for her purse and pulled out the slim, silver box that kept her business cards fresh. She plucked one out and handed it to the glowering man.

"This proves nothing! You could have had this made up for the interview."

True, but that was a little more trouble than a simple reporter would go to for a story on a missing teen. There was probably more than a hundred that went missing every year from the moderate-sized city. Some took off for Hollywood, a few for New York, some for Florida, and a tiny number ran off with their much older boyfriends to live in some isolated area where they would never be found. A few were sucked in by online ads to become models or actresses, which were little more than fronts for prostitution.

She pointed to the card in his hand. "Look up the website."

"Anyone could put up a website." He grumbled as he pulled out his smartphone and typed in the URL. A few seconds of silence ensued as he waited for the website to come up. "Okay, you got a website."

"Scroll down and you'll see all the services we offer. There's even a recommendation from the Indianapolis Police Department." It wasn't actually from the department but from her father.

"I don't see anything about missing people on here. The police captain has the same name as you. Any relation?"

Talk about observant. Her father would so approve of the man and his observational skills. "My first case was a missing person case." She didn't bother to add the man had been dead as opposed to missing. It felt like the wrong thing to say. "I solved it. As for the police captain, he's my father."

The admittance to the relationship status somehow reassured Leon, who smiled. "I can't imagine a police captain lying online for a service. I can see him hawking his daughter's business."

It was hard to know how to take his statement. Did he imply her father may have lied on her behalf? She hoped not. All she could do was move forward. "As I told your wife, we are investigating this case on Tawnee's request. A current photo of Ashlee would be useful. If you wouldn't mind, something that has Ashlee's scent on it for our investigative dog to follow would help, too."

"Dog! You have a dog with you. Where is it?"

It was hard to say if the man planned on picking up Max and tossing him off the property.

Noreen patted her husband's arm. "Leon served with the K-9 unit in the Army. He has a real interest in working dogs."

"Where is your teammate?"

He should be in the back yard with their dog, Chance. With his recent escape into her car to elude the territorial cat, nothing would surprise her.

Luckily, Noreen answered the question. "He's in the back yard with Chance."

The man's mouth dropped open. "He's a working dog, not an overfed pet like Ashlee's mutt. Well, let's go meet your associate."

Max would love to hear himself referred to as a teammate and an associate. Maybe a little too much. Leon led the way, but Noreen peeled off in the hallway. "I'm going to get you a picture and some clothing."

Great. That left them with Sergeant Grumpy. In many ways, he was similar to her father. Often people didn't see past her father's stern persona to the big softie he was inside. However, it would be hard to use the word *softie* in conjunction with the man in front of them. He opened a side door that led to a huge yard complete with a patio that had better outdoor furniture than Nala had in her house.

"Wow!" Elvin exclaimed and gestured to an outdoor television mounted into the exterior wall. "You got a gas firepit, too. You can enjoy the Colts games outside and it would be almost like being there."

Leon chuckled. "Yes. Somewhat. Without being scrunched up to the person next to you and better snacks."

At least the man hadn't pointed out that the Colts played inside a stadium as opposed to the outdoors. Elvin was not the most sports-minded person around. The arrival of people had the two dogs that were actually playing, stop. Max made his way to the patio, while Chance stopped before reaching it. He hung his head, then lay down.

Max walked up to Leon and sat with his head up at attention as her father had taught him.

"Look!" Leon exclaimed with a wide grin. "He recognizes my natural authority."

Not hardly. Nala knew the dog was working the newcomer. It was hard to explain his inherent ability to sense when someone was a soft touch when it came to dogs. All she knew was he had it in spades. He must have developed this ability due to how his earlier life had been checkered with constant rejections that had sent him to the shelter. It may have been due to these rejections that he could sense a dog lover from a distance.

"Yes," Nala pretended to agree. "He's good like that."

"A shepherd, too." Leon reached to pet Max on the head. "They are some of the best working dogs."

No need to admit that while Max looked like a shepherd, there was no way to know his bloodline. "He's a smart one."

"What does he do for you? I've never heard of any shepherds being trackers. They usually use bloodhounds for that."

What did Max do? Talking to other dogs didn't seem like a good answer. "He follows and retains a suspect when needed. He also protects me. He does surveillance work using a camera hooked to his collar. If given the scent, he can find people or pets. We've done a missing pet case in the past." Missing pets sounded so trivial—she quickly recovered. "It was a very important show dog."

She had trotted out everything she could remember Max doing except for eavesdropping and relaying a conversation. People never stopped to think about talking in front of a dog. It felt like she was selling Leon on Max. Elvin must have thought so too and added, "He can tell if people are lying."

"Really?" The man's eyebrows went up. "Show me."

This was not what she wanted. There was a reason she was the one who worked with people and Elvin was the behind the scenes guy. Max could hear. He knew what was going on, which was a plus. "He barks once for truth and twice for a lie. Start with a true statement."

"Ashlee is missing."

Max barked once.

Before she could ask him to state an untruth, Leon spoke slowly and thoughtfully.

"I never cared about her. I never treated her as if she were my own flesh and blood."

Max barked twice.

Leon clapped his hands together. "Correct. I have a much better feeling about you two, knowing you are working with such a capable dog. I'll be willing to pay you well if you could just get Ashlee back home."

Chapter Fourteen

BACK IN THE car and on their way to the university, Elvin cleared his throat, his classic approach to getting attention before he spoke.

"Go on," Nala prompted.

"How do you like that? Max vetted us. That dude thought we weren't on the level until Max was brought into the picture."

"Not exactly. I think he was coming around when he saw the website. Sure, anyone can put up a website, but you actually made me a stellar one. No one who decided to throw one up in thirty minutes could have done that."

"Yeah," Elvin agreed and sunk back in his seat. If there had been enough room in the car, he'd probably have put his feet on the dash and put his hands behind his head. "The website is awesome, especially the animation."

The animation was the part she didn't like. The running lights around the words *now accepting clients* made it look like a cross between a Blue Light Special and a shady check cashing place, although most of those places were shady. She had tried to discourage the extra flourishes but had not succeeded. It was free. She'd tolerate it until she could convince him to change it without hurting his feelings.

"I think he really cares about Ashlee. Most teenagers think their parents are jerks out to make life miserable. I'm sure it's worse for stepparents. They always have to hear about how they're not the real parents while the child fantasized about the biological parent swooping in and giving them a fairytale lifestyle."

"Does that ever happen?"

She shrugged. She knew no one who had experienced it. "Maybe in books, possibly in movies, which is enough for kids to keep dreaming. It's right up there with the perfect boyfriend."

"Hey!" Elvin pointed to himself.

"I'm sure your Abby thinks you're great. You're a reality, not the mythical boyfriend."

She made a few turns and headed up the winding road to the university before Elvin spoke.

"Okay, tell me about the mythical boyfriend that every girl dreams of."

"Not every girl, just most of them. First, he's classically handsome with a tiny flaw that keeps him from being too handsome. Maybe a crooked smile or a bump in his nose. He's not cocky about his appearance, either."

"That could be anyone."

"Not done by a long shot. He's a humanitarian, too. He could be a skilled surgeon who flies to third world countries and works on orphans free of charge."

"How can he afford to do that?"

"He's a millionaire. No, make that a billionaire. With the cost of everything going up, the income of the mythical boyfriend does, too."

"This is unbelievable! No one is like that."

"True, but I haven't even got to the best part. He's a hopeless romantic, who not only writes poetry to his beloved but also whisks her away to exotic destinations in his private jet."

She could go on about the mythical boyfriend's dancing skills and royalty, but she stopped, not because Elvin was making gagging sounds, but because they had arrived at the school. She parked next to her car. "Let's go get Teddy. I feel bad about leaving him alone so long."

"Not sure why. I'm sure Regina leaves him alone all day, and he survives. We were gone at the most four hours. I'm sure he's just waking up after taking a long nap."

She turned off the engine, handed the keys to Elvin, then swung open her door. Luckily, Elvin opened the back door before Max could clamber over the seat. You'd think he was always left in the car the way he shot out whenever the car door opened. "Can you take Teddy back, since you're so good with him?"

"Not to mention you don't want the canine-feline version of World War Three in your car."

"That, too."

They strolled to the offices with Max keeping close. Sure, she should put him on his leash, but he had been confined enough for the day. Most of the students had gone home or to their dorms. The rest were in a late afternoon class. In the distance, she could see a couple holding hands making their way to the lake. No worries about them reporting her for lack of a leash. They only had eyes for each other.

"I feel guilty leaving that pampered kitty in the office."

"He could use some change in his life. Personally, I feel sorry for cats that live locked up in a house or apartment never seeing anything except for their annual visit to the vet. Think of this as a day trip for the old fellow."

Elvin made it sound almost like she was doing the cat a favor. "Do you think he caught any mice?"

"Only if he rolled over on them in his sleep." They both laughed at the possibility.

When they entered the building, David popped out of his office.

"So glad you're here. There's been a terrible racket coming from the office. I wasn't sure if I should get security. I thought at first it could be the telly. I'm not sure if Regina even has one."

The fact he didn't know if Regina had a television in her office meant the man had never been inside. That meant the relationship had to be very minimal or only one-sided in Regina's eyes.

"That must be Teddy. I brought him to deal with the mouse problem. Now, let's see how he's done."

She fit the key in the door and hesitated in turning the knob. An angry cat might shoot out the opening. "Elvin, be ready. Make sure the outside door isn't open."

"Got it, boss."

She cracked the door the tiniest sliver and was aware of David, Elvin, and Max crowding her to see inside. The blinds were up, letting in the afternoon sunlight. It was quiet. No cat running, screaming at them. All she could hear was the sound of chewing. What could Teddy be eating? She crept into the room and rounded a still standing tower of books. Teddy glanced up with a mouse tail hanging out of his mouth.

"Yuk." She stumbled back a step. "I wanted them gone but didn't want to know the details."

Elvin and David entered the room to see what was causing such a reaction.

The proper Brit wrinkled his nose. "That creature is a killing machine."

"Looks like there's two, three, four," Elvin counted the dead mice laid out in a row as if in a mouse morgue. "There're eight mice, and those are the ones he hasn't eaten."

The sight of the mice had her turning to the door and covering her mouth. "Could you take Teddy and the mice out of here?"

"Never thought I'd see the day when you turned all female on me." Elvin joked as he moved forward and swept up Teddy.

"Don't forget the mice," she reminded. The female remark bothered her, but she blamed herself for the mouse massacre. It had been much better in theory than in reality.

"No worries." David scurried around her. "I'll take care of those in a jiffy." And he did.

Watching the Englishman use a dustpan and a trashcan to dispose of the mice was awkward, but on the other hand, it would have been rude to leave while he did so. As he moved toward her with the trashcan, she took a step back.

"I appreciate your help and all. It should be on me, but even though I brought about their demise in the form of Teddy, I still have problems looking into their cold dead eyes."

He wrinkled his nose as he passed. "Strange attitude for a private investigator."

It wasn't the first time she'd heard that comment. People must think a private eye was a combination between special ops and Rambo. "I don't investigate mice, nor do I wrestle people to the ground. I mean, not too much. There may have been one or two times."

It sounded like the congenial man muttered something under his breath as he strolled down the hallway looking for a place to dispose of the unfortunate rodents.

Elvin came in close to her with the cat under one arm. "It looks like you have an admirer. I never did pest disposal for *any* female. Tell you what. I'll head out to Regina's to give the three of you some time alone."

Her friend took off before she could reply.

"I see your friend has left with the mouse slayer," David said as he returned.

"He has." Way to state the obvious. "He's much better with cats than I am. I'm more of a dog person."

"I gathered." He nodded in the direction of Max. "I assumed your friend was the reason you missed lunch."

Rum balls! He *had* said something about meeting for lunch, but she'd spent the day chasing around town after Wyn. "Was that today?" Her hand clamped onto the back of her neck. It was her go-to gesture when she screwed up big. "I got involved in my case. Whoa, I don't know what to say."

His eyes sparkled at her awkwardness. "You and cat boy aren't, you know…" He threaded his fingers together.

"No, never. We're not a couple. We work together. Fake laughing at all his lame jokes would probably kill me if we were, which I don't have to worry about, since we're not a couple." She forced a laugh, then stopped when she realized her comment hadn't been funny. "See, I'm awful at it."

"I have to agree. You could make it up to me?"

The gleam bouncing off his glasses she assumed was from the

overhead lights and nothing else. "We could try lunch again." It would also give her a chance to ask the pertinent questions to see where he stood on Regina. His asking her out for lunch, taking care of her mice disposal, and never having been in her office before pretty much said it all. Still, she needed to know where he was on the book. Was he writing his own or still conferring with Regina? "How about it?"

"Thursday? One pm. Let's try for La Hacienda again."

"Sounds ducky." She thought that sounded British enough. David smirked and waved as she pulled the office door closed.

"I'll see you tomorrow and will remind you just in case."

"You do that." She slapped her leg indicating Max should come. The shepherd was quiet all the way to the car, surprisingly. He'd had very little chance to talk all day. It would be interesting to know what Ashlee's dog thought about her disappearance.

Nala closed the passenger door after Max hopped in, then walked to the driver's side. As she slid into the car, her pooch gave an all over shudder.

"What's wrong?"

"That man. The one who talks funny. He tries too hard. Women don't like that."

Well, it *had* seemed a little needy to her. She closed her door and reached for her seatbelt. "You know this how?"

"I watch television."

"Of course. You can be quite the talk show junkie. Was this the Oxygen network?"

He cocked his head as if perplexed, then shook it. "I can't remember. It was a dating show. You go on the show, then you go out with three guys, then you rate them. The one who did too much was a turn-off for Yolanda."

"I'm not Yolanda."

"Maybe you should sign up to be on the show."

"No." It didn't take her more than a second to reject the idea of public humiliation via reality television. "I better not get a call from the studio, either."

Thanks to her father's efforts, Max could dial 911 on the over-sized desk phone made for medical assistance dogs.

"I won't," he answered and pouted as the engine sprung to life. "If you do get a call from the television station, it wasn't me. Do you want to hear what their dog, Chance, had to say?"

Call from the station? What had he done now? First, he figured out he could command the cell phone by talking to it. She changed her password after that.

That was just about enough excitement for her, except she needed to touch base with the police. They might have no interest, but she did know police didn't take kindly to private investigators usurping their cases, which didn't happen often. Most of her cases never made it to the police because of their nature. If a person felt the need for a private investigator, they wanted things to be discreet. However, if a crime was committed, then information was shared. Her father emphasized she should always mention to clients that she was obligated to report crimes. Too often, one might want a spouse investigated if there were suspicions of fooling around. When it turned out it wasn't a sexy redhead making the husband secretive, but instead, an embezzlement swindle, the client often backpedaled.

"Yes. Tell me what Chance had to say."

"He was sad."

She cut her eyes to Max. He'd told her dog speak wasn't an exact translation, and it dealt more with feelings. "That's it?"

"Very sad. He didn't even want the treats Ashlee's mother gave both of us."

"Anything else?"

"It was delicious." He licked his chops. "I ate Chance's, too. He was okay with it. Why don't you ever get me any quality treats like that?"

"Remember Ashlee? Did he say anything about Ashlee?" Another car swerved around her, which was a good indication she should pay more attention to driving and less to her dog. A quick glance at her rearview mirror didn't yield any other cars coming up fast, but she tapped the gas anyhow.

"Retainer. Chance mentioned that."

"What?" Half the time when she talked to Max, she felt like she'd walked in halfway through the conversation.

"It's something Ashlee puts in her mouth. Chance has chewed up a couple of them before."

Really. Did she need her dog to explain dental appliances to her, especially when she went to the orthodontist for so long? She not only knew all the technicians' names but their children's and dogs' names, too. "Why is this significant?"

"She didn't take it with her. Chance said she wears it every night. If she didn't take it with her, she expected to be back."

All evidence pointed to a girl who may not have made a good choice as far as going out with Wyn, but she had no intentions of leaving town, especially leaving her devoted dog behind.

Chapter Fifteen

THE SUNSET SENT out long golden rays over the autumn landscape as she turned into Regina's neighborhood. Her stop by the local police didn't take as long as she expected, possibly because no one wanted to listen to her. Most of the uniformed officers were helping with a big concert, there was a multi-car pileup on the highway, and someone who wanted to talk about a teenager who went missing in a haunted house didn't rate. The officer on duty took her card and mumbled she'd pass the information on to the appropriate people.

Nala had her doubts. It was obvious the department was stretched thin tonight. Most people assumed their city had endless police on duty. They failed to realize police worked in shifts, officers took vacations, got sick, even took maternity leave. Law Enforcement was one of those jobs where people expected you to show up when they call—yesterday. No one wanted to hear their emergency might be less important than someone else's, which is probably how they rated Ashlee's disappearance.

They *had* put out the Amber Alert, which was more than the other girls got. Tomorrow, possibly tonight, she needed to look into the other girls' disappearances. The easiest way would be to check their social media accounts. The days of disappearing off the grid were much harder. Most people knew enough not to use their credit card and to use cash if they didn't want to be tracked. What they didn't consider was that updating their current status told so much about them.

Millennials and Generation Z-ers could barely breathe without their cell phones. Even when their cell phone or laptop wasn't automatically checking in for them at various locations, casual comments on pictures did that for them. The current love of selfies benefitted the investigative business. A fun shot in front of the iconic Blue Whale meant the person was in Oklahoma on old route 66 or at least near it when the photo was taken. What would have taken hours of asking suspicious people questions that yielded little could be done in under thirty minutes on the Internet.

Some folks were a bit cautious and didn't let just anyone into their feed. Usually, Sawyer got in as a friend by using his fake account, featuring a movie-star handsome photo that usually had all the women clicking accept. His Friendbook wall was composed of various images fed in by other accounts that he created of beautiful people. After Elvin's earlier remark, she considered her own bogus account. She'd identified herself as Holly Go Lightly and included numerous photos of Max.

It might be time for *Holly* to do a little looking. Most social media feeds were fairly open. Not only did the owners want to meet interesting people, but they couldn't help bragging a little about their envy-worth life or at least how they made it appear that way.

"I see the cat is back," Max commented, seeing the rental in the driveway. "He's had time to take the high ground." He let out a blustery dog groan that filled the small car.

What was it with Max and Teddy? If she ever thought for one moment about getting a cat, Max's behavior put an end to such a thought. "Get a grip. I'm sure the old boy is tired after all that work catching mice today."

"Work. Ha!" Max made a derisive sniff. "The mice must have made a suicide pact."

"Come on, it won't hurt to admit that Teddy is good at catching mice. It surprised me, too." She only hoped it didn't have any bad side effects. Pampered pets who had a steady diet of commercialized food did not always do well when they decided to go for a wilder diet.

"I'll admit it to you, but not to him. If that furball puffs up anymore, he won't fit through any of the doorways. I'm surprised he does now."

No reason to point out to Max that he was bigger than Teddy and had no problem getting through the same doorways. She parked beside the rental and noticed no Elvin or cat, which made her wonder where they were. The curtains moved slightly in the front room to reveal a furry face. Obviously, they were inside, but she didn't remember giving Elvin the code. Must have or he wouldn't be inside.

"Let's go." She turned off the ignition, pulled the brake, and swung open the door. Max vaulted over her with his back feet, using her legs to push off from. "Ouch! What did I tell you?"

He went straight to the yard and made use of a nearby tree. She'd have to forgive him. He obviously needed to get out right away. "Okay. I'm heading to the house." She grabbed her purse and headed up the walk. Before she got the door opened, Max was by her side.

"I'm home!" she called out.

Elvin stuck his head into the foyer. "I see. I whipped up some soup and sandwiches for our post investigation talk. Be prepared to be impressed."

"All right." She wasn't all that sure about her friend's cooking skills, but he hadn't starved in all these years of living alone. It beat coming up with supper on her own. However, once she went home, she'd really have to go back to a healthier diet. She closed the door and wandered in the direction of the kitchen.

Max's ears were up as he swiveled his head, inspecting each square foot in search of a certain cat.

"Where's Teddy?"

"Oh, he's on the back porch, watching birds. I think his experience with mice awoke the wild beast inside him."

Max groaned audibly.

Elvin gave Nala a double take. "Why should you care? He's not your cat."

"I'm not sure he's supposed to be outside. He might run away. I better go get him." The last thing she needed was to lose Regina's cat.

Another hearty groan filled the kitchen. "Seriously." Elvin put down the parsley he was cutting over the soup. "I'll go get him. No need for the dramatics."

The back screen door slapped as Elvin exited, and Nala gave her canine a significant look.

"Would it had been terrible to leave him outside? He'd be camping. People love that stuff."

The sound of the door stopped whatever else Max was going to say.

Elvin cradled the cat in his arms. "I bet Teddy is tired and ready for a long nap," he cooed to the animal. He bent and placed the cat on the floor with care.

"Why don't you have a cat? You obviously love them." Nala reflected.

"Ha! I love goats, too, but I don't have any of those in my house. Cat hair and electronics are not a good mix. Let's eat before the soup gets cold. Besides, I get all the cat interaction I want with my girlfriend's pet."

"True. I forgot about Bruno."

"How could you?" Max murmured from his spot under the table.

In the midst of lifting a spoon of soup to his lips, Elvin stopped and sighed. "I know you think that ventriloquist act is cute, but it's getting old. If you try it on any of your dates, it would explain why you're single."

"I don't." Everyone thought being single was such a problem. Did no one ever think she wanted to be single? She picked up her sandwich and bit into it with a little more vigor than necessary. What she thought was regular ham and cheese, had something different about it. "What's in this sandwich?

"Vegemite."

"That is?"

"Something that is big down under. It was in the clearance aisle at Kroger. Quite the gourmet treat, huh?"

Normally, she preferred to know what she was eating. Snicker-doodles! When did she turn into her father? She forced herself to take another bite and chewed. Not bad. It overpowered the cheese and ham. It was good to stretch her dietary horizons. Her cell phone rang before she could decide what vegemite resembled most.

"Nala Bonne here."

Elvin grimaced when she picked up during a meal.

"The séance is on," Tawnee relayed. "Tonight at eleven. It will take us a while to set up. Aunt Belinda asked me to tell you to leave your disbelief at home."

Wow. Maybe the woman *was* psychic. "Will do."

Nala disconnected the call and arched her eyebrows. "Looks like you might be able to knock an item off your bucket list."

Elvin put down his sandwich, grinned, and asked, "You know someone who's able to pull some strings, so I can be at the Indianapolis Colts Cheerleader try-outs?"

"Nope." She shook her head. Even though it might be a private fantasy for more than one Hoosier guy, she couldn't resist teasing. "I'm sure your girlfriend would love to hear about that."

He waved his hands as if trying to erase his previous statement. "Ah, you wouldn't do that. I know women are supposed to stick together and all, but we're work pals."

His comment made her laugh. "I wish women *did* stick together. Some do. Some don't. I'm sure Abby wouldn't go ballistic about your cheerleader fantasy since she's a reasonable female. All the same, I'm sure it would never come up in conversation. About the only time I see her is when I'm with you. It's not like she's going to corner me in the bathroom and ask me to recite your bucket list."

"If she does—"

"Don't worry. I wouldn't cause trouble for a colleague who's such a help." Nala slid back into her chair and smirked before continuing her meal.

"Oh, I know that look. It's the one when you ask me to do something hard or impossible."

"Hey, it's *your* bucket list. We have a séance tonight. I was told to check my unbelief at the door. Who knows? You may see a ghost."

"You won't?"

"Not planning on it. Before we go, we need to look up the names of the girls who are supposedly missing. I should have asked Tawnee while she was on the phone. Brownies!" She slapped the table. Why was it she always thought of things after the fact? This trait wasn't an issue when working with preschoolers. They never had a clue if she'd skipped anything. "Anyhow, I have a plan, which I will admit I stole from Sawyer."

"When's the séance?"

"We're supposed to be there at eleven to set up."

"Set up?" Elvin wrinkled his nose. "What is there to set up? You turn on the red light and the spirits come."

"I'm not sure how to tell you this, but you are confusing professions."

"Want to bet on it?"

Why not? It was a sure thing. "What do you want to bet?"

"Lunch at Bluebeard's, loser's treat."

It was one of the best restaurants in Indianapolis, and it was far from cheap. "That might be a little rich for your blood."

"I'm not worried."

Suddenly, she was. Elvin happened to be one of the smartest people she knew. What he didn't know, he could find out easily enough, and suddenly he was all gung-ho about this red-light stuff.

Not good. "Why do the spirits like the red light?"

"Not sure. I think it has something to do with the root chakra, but it might just be the color that's easiest to see."

"Oh." Well, she didn't know much about spirits or séances. Why take a chance? "I think I'll pass on the bet. We'll start on the girls, and you have the list. I'll boot up the computer." Her laptop was already on the table, she just pushed the power key.

"I sent the list to your email."

"Right you are." She opened up the email she had scanned previously. "The first name on it is Ellie Lawton. I remember Tawnee mentioning her. She was going to New York or something. At least, that was the talk. Maybe to be a model. Not sure about everything you can do in New York City. They have a great culinary school, but I don't think it was that."

"I'm on it." Elvin reached for Nala's laptop and turned it toward him. Fast tapping sounded, followed by a grunt, and then, "Voila!" Elvin turned the computer so Nala could see an attractive blonde in very short cutoffs perched on a tractor. It was a picture from a newspaper.

"Miss Ellie Lawton demonstrates the basic tractor riding form to an appreciative audience at the Columbus Farm Machinery Show." She pointed at the image. "I bet they were appreciative. It doesn't look like she made it to New York, but she *is* modeling, in a way. Okay, next on the list is Joanie Mills, disappeared on September third. Wait! It mentions on your list that she was found on September third, too."

"That one was a hoot. Apparently, her parents declared she was missing, because she was grounded and was supposed to be home."

"You found this out how?"

He pointed to the computer. "Friendbook." He placed one hand on his hip and shook a finger in Nala's direction. "Let me tell you that girl can rant, girlfriend."

"No, don't go there. You stole my plan. I was going to look up stuff on Friendbook and FastSnap."

"Please. That was Sawyer's big strategy. Every middle schooler knows if you want information, search the social feeds. Apparently, all those folks claiming disability while skydiving, dancing with Chippendale dancers, and posting videos of themselves jumping on trampolines have no clue."

"There are those. Are all the feeds public? Sawyer has a bogus account with safe friends on it. All very glamorous and fun, which makes people want to be his friend. He usually waits a while after he busts them to unfriend so they don't make the connection."

"Not a bad plan. I usually read what I can and sometimes hack in, which is not as hard as Friendbook security makes it out to be. Never been caught and apparently no one else has been, either. I may have to make myself a bogus account. You got one?"

"Holly Go Lightly."

"I think that was from Breakfast at Tiffany's."

"You're the only one to make the connection."

"Not even Sawyer?"

"Let's move on to the next missing person, Christine Affton."

Sometimes Elvin could have the tenacity of a snapping turtle when it came to ferreting out information. Most of the time it served her well. As far as Sawyer went, she didn't want to talk about their relationship, business or otherwise. It was bad enough that every single, attractive male that came into her vicinity was immediately judged for his suitability for the family line, the end of which she represented.

Her father had even gone so far as to ask dates if they were okay with hyphenated names, claiming it would be a shame for a child to lose out on the family heritage associated with the name.

"Ha! Sawyer didn't get the reference. I guess he isn't as sophisticated as moi." Elvin pointed back to himself with his thumb.

"No one is as sophisticated as you. What about Christine?"

Fast typing answered, a grumble, which sounded like a dead end, and some more typing. "Another miracle from the sophisticated hacker. I present, Christine Nabors!"

Nala leaned over to see the computer screen where a grinning, and very pregnant, young woman displayed her left hand which bore a wedding ring. Beside her stood a much older man with a pleased expression on his face. "Is that her father?"

"Nope. That would be her chemistry teacher. Apparently, they headed to Minnesota where Christine could marry her teacher without parental consent."

"I never felt that way about *my* chemistry teacher." She narrowed her eyes. "He could be my teacher. So far, we have one would-be model, one girl who didn't run away, another who married her teacher, and Tawnee was so sure that five girls were missing."

"Welcome to the real world. Teenagers make stuff up. Sometimes, they make up stuff to hide the truth, which I'm sure Christine did."

If she didn't stop him, he'd go on about teenage antics as if he were the expert. "I know kids make stuff up. Preschoolers make stuff up, too. I was only going on what Tawnee said. *She* was going on what she heard. Most people hear the beginning of the story, but they seldom hear the ending. Sometimes they don't care to hear the ending, but whether it's four or five girls, I have no doubt that Ashlee is missing. Her best friend knows she had no plans to leave, despite her stepfather being a dictator. Besides, she didn't take her retainer."

"Why does that matter?" Elvin reached back and rubbed his neck as he waited for an answer.

"You have to wear those things every night. Anyone who has braces wouldn't be willing to take a chance on their teeth moving back to their old position."

"Maybe not. What if it was an impulsive action?"

That thought had occurred to her, too. "It would be out of character for a classic overachiever who had skipped a grade. Wyn was still here, so she hadn't taken off with him. I'm not seeing it. I think the lead is Wyn. He doesn't strike me as overly bright, despite his mother's belief he's deserving of a scholarship."

"That was a weird conversation in the hobby shop. It sounded like someone wanted Wyn to come to the house, preferably with Ashlee."

"My thoughts, too. I tried to get the police in on it, but they were busy with a concert and a traffic accident. The officer on duty took my card and said someone would call me. I'm thinking not. Until now, I never realized how much pull the Bonne name had in Indianapolis. Most people on the force knew I was Captain Bonne's daughter and because of it, they *did* listen to me. Not here. Here, they just think I'm a crank with a dog."

"Maybe we'll get some info at the séance."

She couldn't believe her friend just said that. "Do I know you? What have you done with my friend?"

"Remember…" Elvin held up his index finger and pointed. "…you promised to check your disbelief at the door."

Nala shook her finger in Elvin's direction. "Correction, I was told to check my disbelief. I'm going in with a Missouri attitude. I have to be shown, and if I am, well, I'll just have to tweak a few of my stances."

Chapter Sixteen

WITH THE INTENTION of returning back to his hotel after the seance, Elvin took his own car while Nala and Max took the beetle. It was no surprise Max wasn't happy about the return trip to the haunted house. Most dogs liked to nap, and Max was no exception. He was usually asleep before Nala was.

"Why do we have to go anywhere in the middle of the night?" he grumbled. "We should be asleep."

"I agree." The prospect of snuggling into Regina's comfy guest bed with the down comforter and plush pillows was much more of a temptation than driving across town to trespass in a house she did not want to be in to attend a séance she didn't want any part of.

"So, why are we in the car?"

"There might be a clue we missed."

"Like what? Maybe someone nailed a ransom note to the door?"

"Yeah." She gave a derisive sniff. "That would make things easier. The police might be a little more interested, too. I don't think it will happen. We humans will sit down, possibly around a table, and hold hands while Belinda tries to contact some dead guy."

"I notice the use of the word *humans*. Should I ask what I'll be doing?"

Those who thought dogs weren't observant never had one who

could talk. Instead of answering, she wove her way through the deserted streets. Clouds scudded across the moon while the wind rattled the remaining leaves on the trees. If this was the opening of a Halloween show, there would be a lone howl or an ominous cackle. The narrator would come on and add, in a dramatic voice, that some creatures didn't know when to stay indoors, the implication being that those who went outside would experience a calamity of a horrifying nature. At least Max would think so when she told him what she wanted him to do.

"I didn't hear you," Max added.

"Probably because I didn't say anything. As my investigative colleague, I need you to check out the place. Give it a good sniff to see if you can pick up traces of Ashlee."

"Tawnee found her shoeprint and earring. Why do I have to inhale all that dust, mouse droppings, and whatever else?"

"I need confirmation from an unbiased source. It's obvious she wants to find her friend and believes her friend was going there. The police would take you following a scent more serious than Tawnee finding an earring that could have been Ashlee's."

"The police would value my nose over jewelry identification." A huge doggy grin broke out over his face.

Actually, she wasn't totally sure about that but believed in using all her resources. Her father would do more than raise an eyebrow if a she didn't confirm information no matter what the source. "You'll even get to try out some new equipment I purchased just for my canine super-sleuth dog."

"That's me. Glad you finally realized how important I am to the agency. Did you get me a bulletproof vest?"

Even though the work they did was seldom dangerous, Max

harped on getting a bulletproof vest. Police and military dogs had them, so he wanted one. He viewed it as the mark of a canine hero. The vests were probably quite heavy. She'd heard her father complain about the weight on more than one occasion. When the nagging had hit a high, she looked into one. Five hundred dollars, and that was the cheapest. No wonder pet shops had collection cartons on their counter for donations to buy vests for the local canine unit.

"It's not a vest. Something better. A mobile camera with a light. You wear it like a cap like a real officer, and it records everywhere you've been. Police dogs wear them." Fortunately, GoPro cameras were much cheaper for pets than humans. With a little help from the officer who worked with a canine unit, she was able to attach the camera with the motion sensor light to a head harness. The idea of a head harness was to allow the handler to see everything the dog saw. A low hanging collar camera would only catch the floor or anything near it. If Max looked up when a person entered the room, she'd get an image of the person.

The flip side would be if anyone saw Max in his spiffy headdress, they'd assume he was doing surveillance. A well-fed dog like Max wouldn't be wandering through an abandoned house anyhow. If spotted, he'd have to take evasive action.

She parked past the house. If they needed to make a fast exit, the police would block the front of the house. She'd need to plan an exit route just in case. Max hadn't said anything about the equipment, which was odd.

"Didn't you hear me say I got you some actual spy headgear?"

"I did." He twisted to look in her direction. "I think we'll need some promo shots for the website."

That again. "I told you as a private investigator the secret is to be unrecognizable. You would be easy enough to spot with your natural good looks and proud carriage." It was what Max wanted to hear and truthfully, he *was* a handsome canine. She slid into a spot next to the curb, then glanced back in the mirror. No bobbing flashlights or illuminated windows in the house. Had she mistaken the time? She turned off the engine and reached for an oversized LED flashlight, which was supposed to double as a weapon.

"Time to go. Do you want to put your halter on here or wait until we get inside?"

"Now!" Max gave a bark for emphasis.

Of course, she should have known. It was in the back seat. She maneuvered to extract it, only pulling one muscle. "Got it." She gasped out the words. "There's a lot of straps. It looks somewhat difficult to put on, rather like a sports bra."

"Sports bra?"

He was a lot like a kid in so many ways. "I didn't say it was a sports bra, only that it was similar to putting one on the first time. After the first use, you'll be a pro."

"If you say so." He stared at the dangling straps in the yellow light cast by the dome fixture.

When she practiced putting the model on the hard-plastic dog head used for training, it was simple. She didn't get any feedback from it, either. She'd opted for the sturdier halter because she thought it would last longer. It resembled a WW1 flying helmet if the pilot had two ears on the top of his head. As she moved closer to Max, he leaned away.

"What are you doing?"

"Trying to place it on your head. I have to get your ears through first before I can buckle it."

"Looks weird. Smells worse." He made an audible sniff and turned his head away.

"It's leather." She didn't know if she should mention it was second hand. Detective stuff didn't come cheap, which was a shame when you consider what the average investigator made. When she became better known, she'd charge more and maybe even hire an assistant.

Max gave it another sniff. "Cow. There's the scent of another dog. Smoker."

"I doubt the dog was a smoker."

"Not the dog. Whoever handled the helmet before you."

Well, the officer who helped her *was* a chain smoker. "Yeah, you're right about that. I assume the smell will dissipate after a while."

"Easy for you to say. You're not putting it close to your nose."

"Here. Let me try to clean it." She pulled a wet wipe from her glove compartment and rubbed it over the head harness, then waved it to dry. "Okay, let's try it."

Max allowed her to slip the harness on and buckled it while his nose twitched. "Citrus smell mixed with stale cigarette smoke. I'm not even sure how I feel about wearing the hide of another animal."

"You had no issues wearing your collar, which is leather. As is the new one Elvin brought you."

"Where's the camera thing?"

Nala smiled, noticing Max refused to comment on the fact he'd been wearing a leather collar forever. "I'll put it on outside the car.

There isn't enough room in here."

She slung on her backpack, pushed her keys into her jeans pocket, then grabbed the camera and light along with her flashlight as she eased out of the car. Max scrambled out after her. In the meager light of the open car door, she attached the camera and light.

At the unexpected weight, Max dropped his head, looking for all the world like a child who had just dropped his ice cream. "It's crushing my skull."

"It's four ounces. Probably weighs less than that Halloween costume headdress you wanted. I guess if this is weighing you down, there's no reason even to think about the costume." Max's head popped up as she expected it would, and it must have been enough motion for the LED light to switch on.

"Hey. I have a headlight! Neat."

"It's for the camera. It won't do you much good to film at night if all we got is a bunch of dark film. It's also good in low light, dark rooms, and stuff."

"Dark rooms?" Max shook his head. The head cam remained in place. "Not sure I like the sound of that."

"I don't know why it would bother you that much. Dogs are supposed to see well at night. That's when your ancestors did their hunting." She shut the car door, then locked it.

"Shows what you know. That must have been a couple thousand years ago before electricity. There's no reason for dogs to be able to see at night anymore."

A sharp metallic sound stopped her reply. It sounded like metal on metal. The kind of sound a hook might make on a metal car, which reminded her of ghost stories she used to read at night under her covers with her flashlight when she was still in grade school. It usually ended with her trembling under the covers, imagining every sound was proof that a decapitated body was roaming downstairs in search of its head, or the serial killer with a hook for a hand had targeted their house.

Any normal kid might have barreled into their parents' bedroom and jumped into bed with them. Not her. For one reason, her parents' room was on the first floor, and they'd be the first victims. Not only that, her mother wouldn't be pleased to discover Nala had been scaring herself silly with ghost stories she'd taken from her mother's bookcase without permission. Sometimes, it was better to face the possible monsters than Gwen Bonne's disapproval.

"Uh…" she stammered and flicked a glance back at her car. The sound came from that area. Around them were bare trees with outstretched arms and another abandoned house. Only that one's roof had fallen in, making it a less likely party spot. A hoot from a nearby tree startled Max and sent him running down the buckled sidewalk, with Nala trying to keep up but failing. Finally, she stopped when a stitch in her side made it hard to breathe.

She pressed her fingers into her side and managed a husky whisper. "Max. Stop."

Thankfully, he did. He even turned, shining his light on her. "Hey. That was fun. It must be what a train feels like."

The sound of running footsteps caused Nala to pivot and turn on her flashlight. There was a reason her father insisted on a curfew of midnight when she was a teen. Weird and dangerous things tended to happen after midnight when common sense had gone to bed. It wasn't even midnight yet.

"I have a gun!" she announced to the approaching runner.

Elvin blinked as he entered the circle of light. "Who doesn't?

Why did you run away from me?" He leaned forward and placed his hands on his thighs to catch his breath.

"I was running after Max. He took off because I think an owl scared him."

After a few hearty gasps, Elvin straightened up. "You could have called your dog back instead of chasing him. You'd never catch him, when he has four legs to your two."

She wasn't sure if that was a fact, but she did know Max could run faster than her. Maybe an Olympic runner could lap her pooch. "Oh yeah. I should have done that."

"I see you put the head cam on Max."

"Yes, I did."

"Obviously, it doesn't slow him down."

"Nope." Nala twisted around and caught the rounded shape of the beetle by the curb. "Where's your car?"

Elvin cut his chin to the right. "I parked it the next street over. I figure if we're keeping a low profile, having a bunch of cars near party mansion would not serve."

"True, but I figure if we have to leave in a hurry, I don't want to be too far away. This way I'll be running into the dark as opposed to into the arms of the local LEOs."

Elvin chuckled. "If I didn't know you better, I'd suspect you had a wasted youth. If you happen to be running with Mr. Shine on here," he gestured to Max, "you'll be easy enough to trace."

"I can turn the light off."

"I figured as much. You could just stay and tell the truth of how you're an investigator and have permission from the owner to be here."

"Yeah, that should work. I could even give them the number. Of course, with my luck, there'll be at least one Swedish speaker on the force."

"Yeah, that's so common in the Midwest. Let's go do this. I take it Max is going to be doing some investigation of his own?" He indicated the house in the distance and that Nala should take the lead. Instead, Max bounded forward, the light bouncing down the path.

Nala nodded but decided to elaborate. "I brought the sweater Ashlee's mother gave me. If nothing else we can confirm if Ashlee was here and which door she left by. It might not be a huge help, but Max might pick up a scent. It hasn't rained since her disappearance. This is literally an inch by inch investigation."

"Yeah." Elvin agreed as Nala shined her flashlight on the broken concrete and walked ahead.

No need to mention billable hours. They both knew they were doing this pro bono. There was a small light on the porch, but because it kept moving, she realized it was Max. Any passer-by might see the bobbing helmet light as confirmation that the place was truly haunted. What she remembered from the place was it was about one step away from crumbling. It would be best to watch her step. She didn't need any broken bones or to be calling EMS from this location.

Something touched her elbow, freezing her in place. There shouldn't be any wildlife that tall. Maybe it was a branch. She peeked over her shoulder almost bumping Elvin with her nose. "You're practically on top of me."

"It's because I don't have a light. When you shine the light in front of you very little comes back to me with your body blocking it."

No way she could block out *all* the light. "What are you trying to say?"

The front door opened a crack, and Tawnee peeked out. "Please keep your voices down. We don't want to attract attention." She opened it a little wider to let them in and petted Max as he pushed by. "A GoPro for dogs. How clever. TJ will be jealous if you catch any ghosts on film."

Max may have tried for a questioning look over his shoulder, but all Nala got was the LED light in the eye. It sure was bright. She blinked a few times to orient herself and proceeded inside. Elvin murmured greetings and clomped in behind her. It was much darker inside with a flare of light every now and then when Max turned the corner.

"Aunt Belinda is waiting in the dining room. We're fortunate the curse kept anyone from removing any furniture." She gestured to the foyer where a red glow came from one of the rooms.

Nala had watched enough horror movies to know you never walked toward the glow. It could be a demon or a flickering fire that featured a gruesome face that wanted to give you dire warnings, but that were more like promises.

"Give me a second." Nala held up a finger, then whistled, calling Max back. She pulled a plastic bag containing Ashlee's sweater from her backpack. She unzipped the bag for Max to take a strong pull. "You know what to do. Check all the rooms. Be careful. I don't know if there are any rotting floorboards."

The canine turned and headed up the stairs, probably starting at the top and working his way down. That just left the séance for the rest of them. *Yay, them*! Wait. She was supposed to leave her disbelief at the door. At best, she could think of it as a learning experience. Her best friend Karly would love the details.

Tawnee guided them into the dining room where Belinda sat at the head of the table with her eyes closed. A camp lantern sat beside her with a red scarf draped over it. Elvin made a big deal of pointing to it. Good thing she hadn't bet anything.

Tawnee sat at the other end of the table, which left a chair on each side. Before sitting, Nala shined her flashlight on the chair, which appeared to be a sturdy colonial wooden chair, looking a little out of place with the interior.

She sat as Belinda spoke. "Turn off your light, please. As you probably guessed the principle spirit of this house is not fond of company. I arrived earlier and have spent the past two hours attempting to reach him and assure him of our intentions not to harm his home or disturb him, but only to track down Ashlee."

Once the room was dark except for the subdued lighting of the camp lantern, Belinda positioned the lantern in front of her, casting a rosy glow on her face, which actually was very flattering. It made Nala wonder if one of the early mediums decided while candlelight was flattering, a rosy glow was even better.

Belinda cleared her throat. "I need you to concentrate on Ashlee. I know this will be easiest for Tawnee. I believe you have a picture of her with you."

Nala wasn't sure if she was talking to her or her niece, but she rummaged through the book bag for the one she had and placed it on the table. Even though the medium's eyes were still closed, she smiled.

"We can name names, but they mean nothing to the spirits who are not acquainted with Ashlee. A photo should help. I will ask my guides to help me. If my voice changes, no worries. It is only my guide coming through."

They sat in the dark for what felt like forever while Nala worked hard to keep her thoughts on Ashlee. Overhead, she could hear the slight shuffling of Max. If she didn't know he was upstairs, she might assume he was a spirit. The possibility made her smile, Then, aware of her thoughts, she switched them to *I believe*, which made her feel a little like that guy from the old sci-fi shows that was always investigating unusual occurrences.

"Welcome, friends," a young, breathy voice came from the direction of Belinda. It sounded more like a five-year-old as opposed to a grown woman. "I'm Penelope, Belinda's joy guide. I will be helping her to reach the other side. There is a surprising number lined up who want to speak tonight."

How many was that? The possibility made Nala want to look at her watch, but that would break the mood. The breathy voice returned, and she was able to watch the medium's lips. Oddly, her face appeared younger somehow. "I have a young lady with me named Mary. She's wearing clothes that are unfamiliar to me, and she is crying."

Why is she crying? Nala thought but didn't dare say anything.

The voice continued. "She's sad."

That went without saying. Nala tried to wrestle her thoughts into submission before she somehow got in trouble. Usually, it was Max causing a ruckus. Come to think of it, she couldn't hear him anymore. That in itself was worrisome.

The high-pitched voice continued. "She's sad because she killed herself thinking her sweetheart was dead. Mary is even angrier over wasting her life when she could have so easily married another. Wait! There's a man shoving his way through the line."

Instead of the child's voice, a deeper, masculine one sounded. "What are you doing in my house? I told you to stay out of my house. Why don't you have any respect for my grief and leave me in peace? I'm tired of the wastrels using my home like a public house for their drunken debauchery."

Surprisingly, Tawnee chose to answer the accusation. In a voice that trembled a little, she explained, "We're trying to find my friend, Ashlee. Her photo is on the table if you could look at it, please. We don't want to disturb you in your grief, but we believe something bad has happened to Ashlee, possibly in this house. Once we can determine what happened, we will leave."

Nala wasn't sure who she should look at and cut her eyes from Tawnee to Belinda. It was hard seeing either in the dark room. It looked as if something shimmering was coming up behind Belinda. It moved across the table, similar to a low-lying cloud.

Belinda's lips moved, and the angry man's voice came again, but he sounded a little less angry. "Pretty girl. She reminds me of my own sweet daughter to a degree. I did see her. She was here with a couple of the wastrels. I didn't understand it. She wasn't like them. One took off with his girlfriend, but another one pushed this girl into a room and locked the door. He left after that, leaving the girl in the room screaming."

Tawnee resumed the role of the questioner. "What happened then?"

"I don't know. I may only be a spirit, but anguish and fear such as your friend was feeling wears on me. I made the decision to leave, but I do know there were those waiting outside to come in. I didn't see them well. I can only assume they took your friend because you can no longer find her."

"She's been kidnapped!" As soon as Nala realized she shouted the words, she covered her mouth with her hand, hoping she hadn't destroyed the mood.

Something directly above them fell on the floor above, creating a huge cacophony and shaking the chandelier that hung above the table. Spirit or no spirit, she had to check on her dog.

Chapter Seventeen

THE CRASH ABOVE their heads sent Nala rushing up the stairs. One step broke under her foot, but she was able to lift her foot before it sunk down into the gaping hole. The blackness surrounded her, getting darker as she went. Her flashlight was downstairs lying on the table where it was doing her absolutely no good. The steps behind her had disappeared into the darkness, and she knew those ahead weren't the most dependable. A whimper from above made her go upward anyway, reaching for a banister and trusting there was a step for her foot as opposed to another hole.

After a few more steps, a glimmer of light shined through a hallway window. It meant she was almost at the landing. Nala breathed in a sigh of relief and sucked in some dust and other things she didn't want to consider that set off a coughing fit. During it, she heard Max say, "I'm in here. Be careful. It's huge."

"What's huge?" There was no answer, which worried her and caused her to vault up the last three steps. The first door to her right was closed. Surely Max couldn't be in there. At home, he often opened doors, but he never closed any, which was normally a point of conflict. If the two of them got out of this place, she'd never complain about opening doors again. "Max, where are you?"

Bark! Bark! It came from the closed door. *Peculiar*. Nala put her hand on the doorknob and hesitated, trying to decide how she should deal with something that was *huge*. Her weapon was downstairs in her backpack. Her father would point out that a weapon is of no use if it isn't within easy access, but most of her clothes didn't hide the bulge of a nine-millimeter handgun. People got spooked when they saw it, certain she was going to rob them or kill them.

She patted her jacket pocket, hoping for a mysterious weapon to materialize. Her fingers encountered a thin cylinder of breath spray, which contained alcohol. If sprayed in the eyes, it would burn and disorient the huge thing for a few seconds. Maybe long enough for the two of them to get out of there. That could work if whatever in there was normal and not some creepy demon or hungry zombie. She tried to quash the thought, but in a home that might as well be a ghost hotel, it was hard knowing what else might be here.

She exchanged hands on the door knob to be able to aim the breath freshener with her right hand. Go for the eyes, if the soulless creature had any. There should also be the element of surprise. What did they say in horror movies? She slammed open the door.

The white light from Max's camera highlighted him perched awkwardly on a fussy stool. Nala waved her arms in a huge arc and squirted the air freshener. "You shall not pass!"

Another whimper sounded, and Max added, "I want it to pass right on out of here, so I can get down. My thighs are cramping."

She didn't see anything. There was a circle of light around Max, but the corners were still dark. Maybe even darker in comparison to the light. A perfect place for a creature to hide. "Begone you foul creature from the demonic pit! I cleanse this room with holy water."

She turned in a slow circle spraying the darkness and giving it a lovely, peppermint cleanse. Nope, she still didn't see anything. Then, something touched her foot. "Brownies!"

She jumped up with both feet. Unfortunately, they landed with a dull thud.

Max slowly got off the stool, front feet first, then the back feet, and stretched. "It's gone." He gave an all over shudder. "I appreciate the help. Did you see it?"

Actually, no, she hadn't. She shook her head as Max pranced around the room illuminating it with his headlamp.

"Good thing. It was huge. I think it was a Norwegian Roof Rat. They weigh around forty pounds. It was bigger than a beagle."

Nothing that size ran out of the room. Something did use her foot to aid its escape, but it wasn't very big. She would have felt a forty pound rat. Her heart gradually slowed its rapid beat and felt less like it was going to jump out of her chest. Just in case, she rested her hand over it to hold it in place. "Roof rats?"

"You need to get educated. Animal Planet."

That explained it. "Anything on Ashlee?"

"Nada. I went over every room and found plenty of scents." He grimaced. "I might need to clean my nostrils. Breath freshener was a nice touch. When did you get it blessed?"

Blessed? Ah, the holy water claim, which always worked in the movies. "I didn't. I figured any inhuman monster wouldn't know that. Think of it as placebo holy water."

"Got it." Max managed a wink. "I imagine you will eventually want to stop by a church and get some actual holy water in case we encounter the undead or something."

"Nala!" A tentative call came from below. It was Elvin. "Are you okay?" There was a pause, followed by footsteps. The beam of a flashlight shone on the hallway wall. "Do you need help?"

It was easy to translate the question by Elvin's tone of voice. He hoped she was fine and didn't require any help. "I'm good. Max and I are coming down."

It didn't take any urging to get her canine to leave the room. As her only source of light, she had no desire to stay in the eerie room on her own. Nala hurried after her dog. The two of them hurried down the stairs, making a point to avoid the hole she'd made earlier, with cool air wafting up from it, carrying tiny specks of light. Had to be dust motes, really big dust motes. The sooner they left, the clearer she could think things out.

They met Elvin a few steps from the first floor. He grinned when he saw them. "I was afraid I might have to be the alpha male and go find you."

Teasing him was tempting, but right now her interest was leaving. Grumpy Man Spirit, as she referred to him in her head, had witnessed a kidnapping. No way she could list a spirit from the beyond as a source, but kidnapping did make sense. No one had heard from Ashlee. There were no updates on her social media that she was off to be a star or see the world. In the selfie nation world, most kids couldn't help bragging a little about such a momentous decision and taking photos along the way.

"Lucky you. We made it down on our own."

"I heard you talking to someone. Did you encounter a spirit up there?"

Her pooch's overheard conversations were often hard to explain. Normally, she just let people think she talked to herself, adding that it was a sign of creativity. All the geniuses did. Elvin had heard that excuse before.

"It was a man's voice," her friend pointed out. "The weird thing is I think I've heard it before."

"It was the voice of an unfortunate resident who refuses to leave. He's afraid to go to the light. Something about what he did in the past." For something she made up on the fly, it sounded reasonable.

"Great."

Not the response she expected. Elvin rushed down the last three steps and turned in the direction of the dining room. "Belinda, we have another one that needs to be directed to the light."

The medium staggered out of the dining room and put a hand out to balance herself against the wall. "I'm sure you do. Getting Alfred across wore me out. If it wasn't for his daughter coming through to help, I doubt it would have happened at all. We've done what we came to do. That's work for another medium—a professional. Let's go."

"Yes," Nala agreed, anxious to leave for a variety of reasons. It also kept everyone from tromping upstairs to find a non-existent spirit. Then again, there could be more than a few spirits up there. Just because she didn't see them or hear them doesn't mean they didn't exist.

The four of them plus Max walked out together. They kept their voices low, not wanting to attract attention. Belinda and Tawnee peeled off first having parked the closest. Obviously, they hadn't thought out their parking strategy. Max pranced ahead, his LED light cutting a path in the dark.

Glad to put the eerie episode behind her, she nudged her friend. "Did you knock off a bucket list item?"

"In a way. I was expecting to see a full-fledged translucent ghost."

"No ghost after I left?"

"Only a spirit, more than one actually. When you left, Alfred, the guy who used to live here, grumbled about dogs being more trouble than they're worth."

Max could get into some messes, but she didn't want to imagine life without him. "He sounds like someone I wouldn't get along with."

"I doubt many people did. Embittered, lonely, stubborn, not exactly traits that would make him lovable. At least his daughter still cared about him enough to come back for him."

This all happened while she was dealing with the huge monster upstairs, which was probably a mouse, possibly a rat, which made a hot shower a definite when she got back to Regina's. The thought of a rodent icked her out. "Could you see the girl?"

"No, not an outline of a person, but suddenly there was this big spill of light into the room, for just a few seconds, then it closed. There was this feeling that everyone had left the room. Spirits, I mean. Belinda, Tawnee, and I were still there. It was weird. Yep, definitely a bucket list item. Too bad you weren't there. It will be hard to tell anyone if I don't have you to back me up."

She shrugged. It would have been nice to have experienced it. "I was upstairs saving my dog. He was perched on a tiny chair, whimpering."

"Not surprised. Dogs, all animals, are sensitive to spirits. Animals react to what is there, while we humans overthink everything."

The rounded beetle came into view. At least she could go to bed as soon as she got home. As tired as she was, it didn't matter if Max chose to sleep with her. "You're probably right. Do you want a ride to your vehicle?"

"Wouldn't turn it down."

She could hear the relief in his voice. He had been hoping she'd offer. Who would want to walk through a spooky neighborhood, especially after witnessing a spirit reunion? "Okay. You tell Max he has to ride in the back. He'll take it better from you."

"Figures. You make me do the dirty work."

Nala unlocked the driver's door, slid in, and reached across to unlock the passenger side. Once everyone was in, she twisted in her seat to remove the camera and light from Max's harness. The harness itself would have to wait until they were at home.

"Next street over?" she inquired as she started the car.

"Yep. Go up and turn left. I'm barely a block away. It's weird there's no streetlights here. It's not like they went out and no one fixed them, either. There are no lampposts. It's as if this section of town was forgotten."

"It feels that way. Now that you marked off your bucket list item, are you heading back in the morning?"

"Do you mind? I think I've done as much as I can for you. Besides, you had a ghost confirm Ashlee has been kidnapped. I'd love to listen in when you explain this to the police."

Her top teeth worried her bottom lip as she considered the possible conversation. "There's no way they'd believe me. I wouldn't get much response when I mention spirit sources, other than possible laughter."

"There's my car. You passed it."

Nala stomped on the brake, then looked behind her. No one. She backed up so Elvin would be closer to his car and stopped. "Next

time don't park your dark car underneath an oddly shaped tree."
Two limbs forked out from the trunk and ended in a series of small
branches, reminiscent of upraised hands beseeching the heavens for
help. "It's creepy."

He answered as he opened his door, scrambled out, and stood,
half-bent at the open door to be able to see Nala. "I'll keep that in
mind." He smirked, then added, "Good luck. I do hope you bring
Ashlee home. Keep me informed. Turns out instead of a haunted
house gobbling up females who made the mistake of coming there, it
was only one girl. Is there anything you need my help with before I
go?" he asked, while Max wiggled into the front.

"I could use some way to trap Wyn, so I could question him."

"Hmmm. He's a slippery one. You need some extra help. Why
don't you pursue being a scholarship person and ask his parents for
help to talk to him? I bet they would tie him down for that."

"Probably. I will try to work in questions about Ashlee."

"You'll think of something. You always do. See ya."

She held up her hand in goodbye. Elvin closed the door and
walked to his car. She waited until the dome light came on in the
rental before leaving. Time to get home and grab a few hours of
sleep before trying to get students to write something. With any
luck, the know-it-all student would be there to tell her what to do.

Her phone rang. Who could that be when it was past midnight
on a weekday?

Chapter Eighteen

THE PHONE RANG again as Nala scrutinized the number. It wasn't one she knew. Her mother had a policy of not answering calls after ten on the land line. Anyone who knew her wouldn't make the mistake of calling then. Her father didn't have that luxury and had his calls directed to his cell. Any call her father got ended up with him leaving in the middle of the night, which might explain her mother's dislike of late-night calls.

The prefix was local. Who knows? The police might actually be calling her back. "Hello?"

"Thank goodness you answered. I didn't know if you would. I hope I didn't get you up. This is Noreen, Ashlee's mother."

Odd that she'd call so late. "I was up. What can I do for you?"

"Trevor, my ex and Ashlee's father, just called." Her voice trembled as she continued. "He got a ransom note. Ashlee's been kidnapped!"

Nala sucked in her lips to prevent herself from saying she already knew. "That's terrible. Of course, I'll come over. Did you call the police?"

"I did. I expect they'll get here before you do. That way you can share information."

If things only worked like that. After ignoring her, she assumed the police would take over, not even bothering to listen to her theories. Not that she had many, but they were starting to firm up. "I'm on my way. See ya." She hung up before she even had a confirmation.

"Okay, Max. Change of plans."

Her dog lifted his head in acknowledgment. "If we're stopping for a well-deserved snack, I approve. There's bound to be a few fast food places around here still open."

"Probably," she agreed. She should have known. That's where Max's mind naturally went. It tended to stay with basics. Eating, sleeping, and watching television, interspersed with the occasional attempt to order pizza on the big block phone. *Thanks, Dad.* She shook her head, thinking she could never explain why she wasn't excited about the phone that would allow Max to call for help if Nala couldn't. "Right now, we need to go back and see Noreen."

She expected complaints or at least a whine.

"That's cool. She might give me some more gourmet dog biscuits. They're made with hand ground peanut butter, organic wheat flour, and bacon from free-range pigs."

"In the time it took for Noreen to let you and Chance out, I doubt she told you the ingredients in the biscuit."

"She didn't, but Chance did. He told me nothing tastes good with Ashlee gone. She's the one who chose him at the shelter. Unlike me, once picked, he never ever had another home. That's why he's so sad. It isn't home without his girl."

"Aw, that's sweet. I want to find Ashlee. She sounds like a nice girl. Maybe we can get a lead on why someone would kidnap her." She started the car and pulled out slowly. Even though she was no longer in the much-trespassed house, it wouldn't serve to be stopped near it. It also wouldn't pay to shoot through any lights, either. The officers who pulled the graveyard shift were never too happy about it.

Some assumed they gave people tickets out of spite. The reality was that there were so few people on the road it was easy to spot the rulebreakers. The last thing she needed was an unnecessary stop by a local LEO to slow her down. As it was, the police might come and go before she arrived. Even though it was a local girl who was kidnapped, the ransom note went to her father in Ohio, which was weird. It meant the kidnapper knew her father and his address as well as Ashlee. The séance inadvertently confirmed she was taken from the house. Wyn served as the Judas goat who took her there. Maybe the police could get more from Ashlee's bad decision, as Nala tended to think of Wyn. Every girl made at least one. Though usually the result was regret, not being kidnapped.

As she navigated the darkened streets, Max was quiet for the longest time, staring out the window. Finally, he spoke. "Chance is upset that no one will let him out to go look for Ashlee. He's certain he could find her. He has a bit of hound in him."

Sometimes she thought Max had taken on a few human tendencies. It sounded like Chance had a few tendencies himself with his absolute belief he could find his beloved owner. What if he could? Scientists were conducting studies all the time, showing pets are much more deeply bonded to us than our actual friends. There were endless stories of dogs finding their way home over thousands of miles. If Chance could find Ashlee, it would just be the process in reverse or maybe the same, since the dog was still finding its owner.

"Do you think he could do it?"

"I do. Most dogs are all bark. This dog has a real heart for his girl. He can do it if given a chance."

A police car was in front of the house with its lights on. Nothing like a police car in front of your house to announce your business. Still, all the neighbors must have heard the Amber Alert. No time to waste. She parked, let Max out, and they walked to the door. Noreen opened it before they could knock.

"I'm glad you're here. Officer Montgomery would like to know what you found out."

She entered with Max at her heels. There was already an officer sitting on the white lounger with the silver report box in his hand. He nodded in her direction. "I see you brought your detective dog, too. I'd be curious to share information."

"Nala Bonne, private investigator." She held out her hand.

He stood and grasped her hand in his. "Officer Montgomery, Brad. I hear you've already been working on this. Tell me what you know."

Here it goes—the sharing of information with a man who had nothing to share. "Okay." She cut her eyes to Noreen who stood near her husband, but swayed from foot to foot, uncertain what to do next. "Could I have a copy of the ransom note?"

"I'll send it to your phone." Her husband handed her the phone, she scrolled, tapped at her keyboard, then Nala's phone chirped, signaling she had received the image. While she enlarged the image and studied every inch of it, what she really wanted to do was send the image to Elvin and get his take on it. Instead, she'd have to explain what she had done so far to Officer Montgomery.

"Tawnee, Ashlee's friend, asked me to look into the disappearance."

"Why didn't you assume it was just a missing person?"

Like you did and all your 'couldn't be bothered buddies'. "Tawnee is Ashlee's best friend. They share each other's secrets. She knew Ashlee was excited about her first year of college and that she had recently broken up with her boyfriend, Cody."

"Yet, her mother tells me she went out with another boy."

The way he said it sounded a little judgy, like girls couldn't go out with boys, especially after breaking up with one. "Even though she broke up with Cody, due to starting college, she still cared about him. She regretted the break up, but felt it was something she needed to do to excel at college."

"It's my fault." Noreen's husband pushed up off the couch. "Cody is a good kid. I just didn't want Ashlee getting too serious so soon. If she hadn't broken up with him, she wouldn't be sneaking out to date this troublemaker."

"It wasn't like she even liked him. She just wanted Cody to hear about it. Tawnee knew it was all about making him jealous. Maybe she thought he'd sweep in before she even went out with Wyn."

Montgomery held up his hand. "This Wyn. Have you talked to him?"

"I have tried, twice. He always seemed to be leaving the scene. I did record him in the hobby shop saying something about being paid to take Ashlee to the haunted house."

Noreen gasped while her husband wrapped an arm around her. Montgomery turned his judgy eyes on her. "Why didn't you contact the police then?"

"I did. Went down to the station, told the officer on duty my business and even gave her my card. At best, she seemed disinterested. Told me it was a busy night with the concert and a big pile-up on the highway. No one called me. I also had confirmation from a reliable source that Wyn *did* take Ashlee to the house and locked her in one of the rooms. Two other individuals took custody of her." No way would she admit a spirit was her reliable source. The spirit had nothing to gain by lying about it.

Noreen shot across the room and grabbed Nala by the shoulders. "When did you find this out?"

"About twenty minutes ago. From what I was told, I assumed she was kidnapped. It wasn't a grab-any-pretty-girl type of thing. Wyn lured Ashlee there for a purpose. I just don't know what it was. Why Ashlee? Why demand ransom from her father and not you?"

She nodded to Leon, who had removed his wife's hands from Nala's shoulders, which was helpful because the woman not only had a strong grip but sharp nails, too. The worried furrows in the man's face deepened as he cleared his throat.

"That was my first thought, too. None of it makes sense to me. Even though he's getting up there in age, Trevor likes to pretend he's in his twenties. He's always running these get rich quick deals. Whenever he makes money, he gambles it away. He rarely comes to see Ashlee, and when he does, it's because he's on his way to the riverboat casino down there by Bridgeport." He spat out the words making no effort to hide his feelings. "At the most, they have dinner together. Now and then, he brings her a cheap trinket he probably bought for the various women he chases. Anyone who knows him would know he wasn't good for the money."

Noreen, who had been clutching her husband with silent tears running down her face, pressed her hand to her heart. "Oh my God! Do you think a loan shark has her? Maybe Trevor owes him money, and this was how he hoped to squeeze money out of him. What if it's the Mafia?"

A loan shark could be a possibility, but not the Mafia. Still, not many loan sharks would cross state lines to kidnap a minor. If caught, they'd be in a lot of trouble. Professional criminals and stupid thugs she could see doing it. The professional would have the confidence and experience to pull it off. The thug wouldn't. Her money was on the thug. They were dumb enough to hire Wyn, who she thought would break like a pistachio shell if pressure was applied.

"We will have to swing by and see him in the morning," Montgomery commented and dropped his eyes back to his notes. "Do you have any more information?"

"I'm betting Wyn will go to ground. If you wait too long, he will have taken off. I'd be surprised if he's even home now. I also believe that Ashlee is somewhere around Floyd County, tucked in an abandoned building, or in an isolated place where no one would hear her cries for help. There may have been a plan to transport her, but thanks to the timely Amber Alert, it nixed that. It didn't stop the ransom plan, though. What's odd is that they contacted the father as opposed to the mother who would do anything to ransom her child."

"That's right," Noreen interjected. "Trevor contacted us because he doesn't have the money. When we were together, he loved to play the ponies and knew he would occasionally make some money. It was usually feast or famine. Someone might have heard he's had some big windfall," she said with a scoff. "They just don't know how fast he could lose one."

Instead of asking the asked for amount, Nala pulled out her phone and brought up the image. The ransom note asked for five hundred thousand dollars in small bills. It was a lot, but she had faith Noreen and her new husband could cough it up. Still, something wasn't right about this whole scenario. It never was when a child was taken. Why the wait before asking for ransom? Worse, how could they know if Ashlee was even still alive?

"We need to go to the Samuelson's house tonight."

Montgomery pointed to her. "You could do it. I can't. If it was a domestic abuse call or a home invasion, I could come in with sirens blaring if the police were called. When it comes to questioning people, that has to be done during normal hours, which isn't after midnight. I know you think he's guilty of being messed up in this, but you can't prove it."

"What about the recording where he says he was paid to get Ashlee. It's in my car." She started for the door and noticed Max had disappeared while they were talking. He probably went to find Chance.

"Did Wyn know you were recording him?"

"Of course not, I was outside the shop. My associate was inside the shop."

"Then, it's inadmissible. Not much you can do with information that was obtained in such a manner."

Really. He was going that route. "I could establish a timeline. Motivation. Possible suspects." Pretty much everything the police hadn't done.

"True. You can knock on the door and wake up the parents. Who are they going to complain to?"

He had a point. She was the boss. There were times when it was good to be the PI.

Chapter Nineteen

THERE HAD BEEN some crazy moments in her short investigative career, including being shot at while weaving through traffic on Highway 465. Those things were spur of the moment. This time, she was driving to the Samuelson's house in the middle of the night. Most likely, they wouldn't answer the door or worse, they'd shoot first, claiming it was a burglar. She'd have to put the camera back on Max so at least there would be a record of her death. She should call Elvin. He should still be up. That way, at least, he'd know where she went and the why behind it. Besides, something was bothering her.

The phone burbled several times before a sleepy "Yo," came over the phone speaker.

"Good. You're up."

"I wasn't up. What's wrong with you? Why are you up?"

"Ransom note." Her eyes were on the approaching headlights, which seemed to be on the wrong side of the road. Could be her eyes were playing tricks on her.

"What? At this time of night? Weird. Where did Noreen and Leon find it?"

"On their phone." She kept her gaze on the road and the approaching headlights that were moving fast. Max erupted in a frenzy of barking as her car lights illuminated the oversized truck coming right at them. Nala pulled hard to the right, taking the beetle onto the gravel shoulder where it came to a shuddering stop mere inches from plunging to the highway running underneath the overpass. Her hand automatically went over to check Max, who miraculously managed to stay rooted to his seat. Not so with the phone that was somewhere in the car.

Elvin's voice questioned from underneath the seat. "What happened?"

Once she retrieved the phone, she took a couple of breaths to settle herself before replying. "Nothing good. Dad warned me that nothing good happened after midnight. I think it also translated that most people out on the road after that time are drunk. Some idiot was speeding down the wrong side of the road and would have killed us if Natalie, my beetle, wasn't so small and my reaction time wasn't so fast."

"Are you and Max okay?"

She ran her hands over her dog checking for any swelling or bruises. "Max seems to be okay. I'm shaken. Personally, I would like to call it a day, but I'm on my way to the Samuelson's house for an ambush interview."

"Police?"

"Nope. They frown on showing up at people's houses in the middle of the night for random questions. Officer Montgomery asked me to go. He figures I can't be fired. I decided to put the head cam on Max in case something happens to me. I have confidence Max can escape."

"I'm not feeling good about this."

"Me, either."

"Want me to come with you?"

"I think I will be less intimidating with just Max."

"Who happens to have a head cam on."

"There is that. Anyhow, I need you to look at the financial paperwork, insurance, taxes, etc. Anything recent relating to Trevor Bolen."

"Ashlee's father?"

"You got it. He's the one who received the ransom, which is peculiar. He lives in Ohio, and Ashlee was taken from Indiana. It's obvious that the mother and her new husband could pay the five hundred thousand. Trevor not so much. In fact, he contacted Noreen to let her know about the ransom to get money from her."

Elvin's whistle blared out of the phone speaker. Max barked as a result. She picked up the phone and took it off speaker—it wasn't like she was driving—and held it up to her ear to hear her friend still speaking. "What did you say?"

"Everything about it is fishy."

"My thoughts, too, which is why I called. Noreen thinks Trevor could have come into big money and someone heard about it and is trying to separate him from it. There's also the chance he owes a lot of gambling money to a loan shark who's trying to get his money back. Get back to me with the information, pronto."

"Tell you what, I'll be at my end doing my magic fingers routine, but leave your phone on. That way, I will hear everything and record it."

"It won't be admissible in court."

"Yeah, yeah, I know. If anything should happen, and I say it won't, I would hand the recording to your father who would make Liam Neeson in *Taken* look like a boy scout."

"It's the role my father has always been prepping to play with his ability to drive any type of wheeled vehicle and fly small aircraft. I'll take care. I wouldn't want him to think all those escape scenarios he put me through were wasted. Okay, I'm putting you in my backpack, but am turning the sound up so you can hear. I'm not that far from the house, and I'm betting they won't answer anyhow."

"Gotcha."

She withdrew her gun and placed it on the dash before inserting the phone into the backpack. The holster her father bought her would have come in handy right about then. Instead, she checked the safety on the gun and inserted it into her sock. People underestimated good quality socks when it came to impromptu gun holsters. She buckled her seatbelt, then started the engine. Do the hard thing and everything should fall into place.

As she drove, she considered Trevor as opposed to her upcoming confrontation. Analyzing behavior sometimes calmed her. Even though Noreen hadn't waxed on about her ex, it was apparent from Leon's remarks that the man didn't try to see his child. Ashlee and her father weren't close, and didn't see each other often. Therefore, it made no sense that someone would snatch his daughter. First, they'd even have to know he had one. Why in the world would they know about her and better yet where she lived and went to school? Someone knew enough to solicit help in the luring of a naïve overachiever, too.

The neighborhood was close, and she cut her speed to not miss the turnoff. The headlights lit up the reflective signs, showing her turn. She knew the house was just before the little bridge. Should she turn off her lights before slipping into a parking spot? There was also the blocking-the-escape-route maneuver, but she couldn't do that to Natalie. It would make getting back to Indy difficult, too.

There was Wyn's jeep, which was a big plus. It meant he was home unless he hitched a ride with someone else. The car eased into a spot behind the jeep, and she turned off the lights.

"Okay, this is it."

Max turned slightly as if questioning if she was talking to him.

"Elvin is on the phone in my backpack, listening." It also let Max know now would not be the best time to start his cheeseburger rant. She continued in double-talk. "I will put the headcam on Max to record any significant action. If shooting should occur, his job is to hide. Elvin will find him. I don't think anything will happen, but we have to plan for the worst-case scenario. That's what survivors do."

She was repeating her father's words. People eventually turned into their parents. She just didn't expect it to occur so soon. She slipped out of her car quietly, being respectful of all the sleeping neighbors. Even Max slunk out of the car without his usual fanfare. They were almost up to the door when a form backed out of the shadows. With the house lights off, it was a little hard to distinguish who it was. A nearby security light allowed her to see the silhouette was slender and masculine—probably not Mr. Samuelson. It was Wyn, she decided, due to his trademark hair and the fact he was sneaking out.

"Going somewhere?" she asked.

The figure spun. "Yes." He straightened to his full height, which wasn't much taller than Nala. "Get out of my yard or I'm calling the police."

"Go ahead. I assume they're already on their way."

"What?' He pivoted to peer down the street for any tell-tale flashing lights. "You're bluffing. What are you, a burglar?" He pointed to Max. "What's up with robo-dog?"

"He's recording you." Good. She managed to get that out there and on tape, which would make the recording legal.

"No." Wyn held up his hands to cover his face. 'I don't have to stand here. I'm going back inside."

The porch light went on and an older man in pajamas and a robe came to the door. "Wyn, what's going on?"

"Nothing, Dad. I was just coming in."

Nala saw the window of opportunity shutting. She reached for her identification and held it out to the man who took it, glanced at it, and handed it back while she talked. "Mr. Samuelson. I'm Nala Bonne, private investigator, looking into the kidnapping of Ashlee Bolen. Your son is the last person to see her, and in all kidnapping cases, time is of the essence, which is why I came so late. A ransom demand was just made. Any information your son could give me may save this young girl's life."

"Wilson," the father uttered the name in a commanding tone, "is this true?"

"Please, Dad," Wyn's voice swung upward into a whine. "It wasn't like that. Some dude wanted to meet Ashlee. He was going to pay me if I got her to the mansion, which I did. That's the last I saw her. Honest."

The father reached out, grabbed the son's arm, and shook him. "What stupidity have you and your worthless friends done now?"

"It was nothing. Like I said, some guy wanted to meet Ashlee. I don't know what happened after that. She could have run away."

Nala pursed her lips before delivering the next verbal blow. "Hard for her to do being locked in a room. You locked her in a room to make it easy for the kidnappers."

Her remark did get a reaction, more than she expected. Wyn shook off his father's grip and lunged at her. Max growled and bared his sharp teeth, bringing the impulsive teen to a dead stop. It might be best to add some more restraints. "Keep in mind, you are being recorded. My dog, Max, is trained to attack if I should signal him to do so, which I would do if I feel threatened."

Wyn was breathing hard, and it was easy to tell what he'd like to do to her. "You can't prove anything."

To which Nala replied, "There was a witness who IDed you. There was not one dude who wanted to meet Ashlee. Two showed up to take her from the house you delivered her to, which makes you an accessory."

"Son, don't say any more. We need to call Uncle James. This is going to kill your mother."

Listening was not one of Wyn's skills. He snarled a reply. "If someone was watching, they were just as guilty as me because they did nothing. This witness could have saved her."

"You could have, too. You still can with any information about the guy who hired you."

He shook his head. "I never got paid. It was more like he tricked me."

"Who was your contact?"

"Sean. He's in my algebra class. We hang out sometimes. He told me he met a dude at his part-time job at the horse track who was super shy and wanted someone to set him up to meet Ashlee. He chose me because he knew I was popular with the ladies."

Actually, he chose him because he was easily duped. All he had to do was appeal to Wyn's vanity. "Do you know Sean's last name?"

His mouth opened as if he would say something, then he closed it. Finally, he shook his head.

"I find it hard to believe you'd hang out with someone whose last name you don't know."

Before Wyn could answer, his father did. "I don't."

Anyway, she got what she came for. "Stay in town, please. The police will want to talk to you in the morning. Nothing shouts guilty like taking off."

Mr. Samuelson called out as she turned to go. "Why did you show up in the middle of the night?"

"Because I can. Every minute counts as far as bringing Ashlee back safely. When I showed up, your son was sneaking out. I imagine he has his getaway bag already in his jeep."

Wyn glared at her. "Don't you have someone else's life to ruin?"

She pretended to look at her watch. "I do. Believe me, I do."

Chapter Twenty

WHEN NALA GOT back into her car, she pulled the phone out of the backpack and spoke into it. "Did you hear?"

"Most of it—even Max's warning growl. Great job mentioning you were recording. Kudos. Dummy Wyn kept on talking."

"It was nice how he blabbed all he knew. I'd like to find this Sean. Might be able to do that by just asking the chancellor. What do you think?"

"It would be easy enough to figure out who the algebra teachers are. Ask who has Wyn and Sean in their class. You start talking to the higher up officials, they'll clam up, all worried about lawsuits."

He made a good point. "You'd think they would want to help find Ashlee."

"They'll work hard not to be associated with it. You might have to wait until a decent time to question anyone else."

Nala replied, "I don't think I can. Every minute counts. It has been too long already."

"They're demanding a ransom."

"There's no proof she's even alive."

"Her father didn't ask?"

"Apparently not. Instead, he just contacted Noreen and Leon for the money."

"Cold."

Nala had thought the same, but then a tiny little niggling in the back of her mind finally formed into a coherent thought. "I got it! You've probably heard about the rich and famous insuring their kids in case they get kidnapped?"

"Yeah, I think I see where you are going with this."

"Sawyer mentioned this to me once. It's a thing now to insure your kid and fake a kidnapping to collect."

"It's a thing? You're kidding me."

The Samuelson's porch light was still on. Mrs. Samuelson had come out, and they were pointing at her. The woman had probably guessed by now her son wasn't getting a scholarship. Time to get out of here. She started the car, trying to decide which way she should go. Couldn't get to Sean yet.

She started back to Ashlee's house as she talked to Elvin. "Nope. It's up there with over-insuring your house and burning it down. Insurance companies are on to this and hire investigators like Sawyer. They'll take money from anyone who wants kidnapping insurance. Paying it out on the policy almost never happens. Contrary to the movies, there aren't that many legitimate kidnappings, or the people who are kidnapped, weren't insured. I guess if kidnapping is a possibility, your kids will probably have body-guards."

A momentary silence made her wonder if the call had been dropped. "Elvin, are you there?"

"I'm here. I'm trying to pull up an insurance database. I'm not even sure who covers that kind of thing."

"Forget about that. Sawyer can look it up without even hacking into a database."

"Sounds good. I'm sure he could do it for you." There was a smile in his voice.

Why wouldn't the man do it for her? They were business partners. "I have another project for you."

"Wait. Let me tell you what I discovered about Trevor. He's busted. Someone accused him for fraud due to his recent business venture. I'm betting he's trying to get funds to fly south to somewhere where he can't be extradited back to the States."

"Sounds about right. I need to pass this information on to Officer Montgomery, who can contact the LEOs in Trevor's part of the world. I'd say the man's a flight risk. We need to find Ashlee before he flies. Remember saying how it felt like the part of town where the haunted house was had been forgotten by the city? Well, it got me thinking that the whole street is vacant. No one goes there, except for the haunted house. If Trevor hired some low rent thugs, they'd try to get by as cheap as they could and do as little as possible. They might even stash Ashlee nearby. I'm going to see if I can get her dog, Chance, and see if we can pick up a scent trail. We left in such a hurry, I didn't even have Max do that. I felt we had confirmation and ran with it. Call me with any known derelict buildings, but they would have to be away from everything else where no one would be around to notice people coming in and out. If things heat up, which they are, I imagine whoever was hired to sit on Ashlee would take off leaving the girl locked up, possibly tied up to die of hunger and dehydration. I'm certain Trevor is our culprit. Right now, I just need to get Ashlee."

"I second that. I'll let you go."

No sooner than she hung up, the phone rang again. She thumbed it on. "I thought you were going to get to work on the case."

"I am…" a male voice that wasn't Elvin's replied. "This is Officer Brad Montgomery. We met earlier. How did the meeting go?"

She relayed the information and the fact that Trevor was being investigated for fraud and was a flight risk.

"I'll get right on it. What're your current plans?"

"I'm picking up Ashlee's dog to search for her along that street where she was last seen. It's been less than three days, and no rain, which mean Chance, her dog, will be better at picking up her scent. I have reason to believe she could be very close."

"If that's the case, I'll see what I can do about bringing in some help. I'll see you down there." He cut the call, which was no surprise. Police never had time for extended goodbyes.

IT HADN'T BEEN too hard to get Ashlee's mother and stepfather to agree to let her use Chance. What she couldn't do was to convince them to stay home. In the process, they woke up other neighbors, who roused their families to help search. Thankfully, none of them insisted on bringing their dogs.

Their ragtag convoy came to a halt in front of the mansion. She attached the camera and light to Max's harness before getting out of her car. He would hate the harness by the time she took it off him. With any luck, they'd have nice calm cases for a while, where she investigated date history or tailed erratic-acting spouses. It was the opposite of exciting, but it was the bread and butter of the agency, and it didn't involve Max wearing headcams.

She climbed out of the car and held up her hand to the crowd that had gathered. "It's still night. In fact, it's only two-thirty. We want to find Ashlee, but we have to keep it calm or the police could be called. I'm going down to the house with Chance to see if we can get a scent trail. The good news is it hasn't rained. Stay here until we get a definite direction to go."

Both Leon and Noreen accompanied her, which she expected. What concerned parent wouldn't be shadowing her steps? Nala had a hold on Chance's lead, and he already had his nose to the ground. By the tugging, she knew he had picked up his owner's scent. He wanted to run, but she held him back. "Conserve your energy. I'm not too sure how long this trail will hold."

"What do you mean?" Noreen asked, her voice tired and thin.

"I know bloodhounds can smell a person traveling in a car with the windows up. Not sure about Chance. I'm counting on his absolute devotion to Ashlee. He might be able to pick up her scent even if her abductors carried her."

The mother shot a grateful glance at the dog pulling Nala down the walk. "When Ashlee picked him, I tried to discourage her. There were much nicer dogs, better-looking ones. She wanted Chance because he was the most pitiful in the batch. Imagine that." A sob caught in her throat.

Leon had a heavy-duty flashlight. Combined with Max's LED light and her own light, they provided enough illumination to see where they were going. They entered the house with little fanfare. It was odd being in the place again. It felt empty. No lingering spirits hanging about, looking over the place. Noreen exclaimed her distaste of the dirt and spiderwebs. Her husband said a few things about what he'd like to do to the culprits.

Chance found the room she'd been locked in and raced around

it with joy. "Good dog." She snagged the lead he'd jerked out of her hand. "Go find Ashlee."

He jerked, sniffed the floor, then lifted his head. He walked slowly down the hall with his nose up in the air. She must have been carried. They exited through the back door and instead of heading for the derelict houses on either side, Chance went for the woods, which caused Nala's heart to tumble. The last thing she wanted was to come across Ashlee's crumpled body with her parents in tow.

On the scent, the determined dog plowed forward through the briars and through the scrub trees. Fearing what might be ahead, she decided to send Max. She whistled, and her dog who was off leash came to her side. She pointed ahead. "Go search!"

Max ran into the darkness, with only his LED light, demonstrating no fear. He could be quite the courageous pooch when he needed to be. Her father had been working with him on search and rescue, certain he had what it took. So far, she and her mother took turns being the victim and would hide or lie on the ground. Max always found them. She wasn't certain what he would do if he found an actual dead body. She heard cadaver dogs often became depressed at only finding dead people.

Even though she told the neighbors to wait, she could tell by the lights over her shoulder they were creeping up from behind. She couldn't blame them. They came to search, not stand by a curb in the dark. There was a bark up ahead. Max had found something! Her father had worked out a code. It was once for a person, twice for danger. He barked again. Was it one bark with a pause, then another bark, or was it two barks? She held up her hand. "I'll go ahead alone."

The flashlight illuminated Noreen's determined face. "Like hell, you will."

Maybe she wouldn't go ahead alone.

Max barked two times in quick succession. It *was* a building. Chance gave a hard tug at the lead, and it broke. The broken lead dangled from her fingertips as Noreen gasped beside her. "We can't lose Chance. Ashlee would never forgive us."

"We won't," she assured the woman. "Max will bring him back."

She only hoped her words would prove true while she broke into a jog, being slashed by sticker bushes and running into cobwebs as she followed Chance's route. Being closer to the ground, he missed most of the natural hazards.

Up ahead, a frenzy of barks erupted. She could pick out both Chance and Max's. Behind them came a long baying she associated with a bloodhound. Someone must have brought one after she asked them not to. Ginger snaps!

Leaves crunched, and branches snapped as Leon and Noreen labored to keep up. Who knows what they would find, but apparently the dogs thought they'd found something. Nala gave a final push to get there first. She broke free of the trees, and the dogs were circling a small outbuilding, barking as they did so. It was odd having a building so far away from the house. She really couldn't figure out what purpose it might have served, but for someone planning on abducting Ashlee, it would be a good place to stow her before moving her somewhere else.

In a burst of adrenaline, she sprinted the final yards, and her hands landed on the shed with a hollow thud. A knock came from inside. To be sure, Nala knocked and heard an answering knock. Someone *was* inside. By the way Chance was whining and pawing at the building, she was sure it was Ashlee. A heavy padlock was attached to the door, and the windows were boarded up. Why didn't she ever put bolt cutters into her detective backpack? Wait! She had something that might work. A shorty crowbar her father joked was the ultimate passkey when he had given it to her earlier.

She shrugged off her pack and located the crowbar. The boarded-up window offered the best opportunity of access. The first board popped off easy, then the second with a little more effort, and then the bar was lifted out of her hands. *What*?

Leon wielded the bar and attacked the boards with a frenzy.

Noreen murmured, "Let him do it. He needs to do it. Let him demonstrate that he's always been her real father."

The tall man threw the broken boards right and left. Bright lights broke through the trees along with more baying from the hound. Chance whimpered near one wall where she was sure Ashlee must be. When Leon created a hole big enough, he dropped his light in, then scrambled after it. "She's here."

There was a pause, then he added, "She's alive!" There was a ripping sound, then a gasp.

A breathy voice came from inside. "Oh G…God, Thank… thank you…for…finding me," Ashlee was barely able to speak in between sobs and gasping for more air.

"We never gave up."

"Wha…What about…Ch-Chance?"

"He's outside. The private investigator that Tawnee hired thought Chance could find you, and he did." A bloodhound came through the trees secured by a long leash, with a man in a flannel shirt, jeans, and a John Deere hat at the other end. Two uniformed policemen jogged out of the woods carrying portable spotlights. One, she recognized as Officer Montgomery.

"We found her! Did you bring some bolt cutters with you?"

The other cop laughed and reached for the bag on his back. "I'd told you we'd need them."

The bloodhound ran up to Nala and bayed long and loud, making her ask. "What scent was the dog following?"

"Yours. We took it from your card. It was nice and fresh. We probably could have followed the rest of the folks who were following you," Montgomery explained while his fellow officer cut the lock off with a loud *crack*.

Leon carried Ashlee while her mother walked close by, continually touching her face and hands as if to assure her that her daughter was still alive.

Max crowded beside Nala, and she bent to pat him on the back. "You're the bravest dog, ever and another successful mission. We need to get back home and get some sleep before I talk about…" She yawned. "…creative writing."

Epilogue

THE BRIGHT SUN made her reach for her sunglasses as she glanced around the restaurant courtyard for David. The smiling Brit stood up just in case she couldn't see him. She'd call him handsome in that unassuming way that English men could pull off. After all, he did dispose of the mice for her, which may have increased his attractiveness. *Think of Regina*, she reminded herself. She also needed to keep to the agenda, too. Her goal was to find out what the man's intentions were toward Regina and her book proposal.

"Hail the conquering heroes!" David stated, causing a few interested stares.

"Stop that." She slid into her seat, and Max found a spot under the table. "I was just doing my job."

"Fill me in on the details."

She laughed. "Yeah, you and everyone else wants to know the details. It's currently an active felony case. If you read the papers, then you know both Ashlee's biological father and her impulse date, Wyn, have been arrested and are in a major trouble. All I can say is Ashlee is back home and has a new respect for her stepfather and his strict rules. Not too surprisingly, Ashlee is back with her old boyfriend. It took a scare of almost dying to bring out her true feelings.

"I can identify with that."

"Really?" This was about to get interesting. David might mention the chemistry he felt when they had first met.

"I've always had a hard time talking to women I have feelings for." His lips went up in an endearing smile.

She pointed back to herself with a thumb. "You've never had an issue talking to me."

"Exactly. You're easy because I would never imagine having a relationship with you. You're all steak and lobster, and I'm a tea and crumpets man."

Well, this had to be the most delicate letdown in romance history. "So, why did you ask me to lunch?"

His brows knitted together. "To eat lunch. It's like I said, you don't know anyone at the university. Besides, Regina asked me to do it. I could never refuse her anything."

The dopey expression, she assumed, was for Regina. It sure would have been nice if Regina had mentioned she asked David to offer a lunch invitation. Of course, it was probably part of her plan to find out the man's intentions. A waiter showed up and asked for drink selections. David asked for hot water and had brought his own tea bag. She opted for a margarita.

"Celebrating solving the case?" David asked after the waiter left.

"Something like that. So, David, you have a crush on my friend. It's my job to determine if your intentions are honorable. What's up with you collaborating with her on her book?" Sure, there were probably better ways to ask, but she was tired and ready to go home after she consumed her margarita and quesadillas.

"Oh, you heard about the book. You two must be very good friends indeed. I pretended to be interested to spend time with her. I think it's going to be an outstanding book. My name should not be on it. Quite frankly, I did nothing but let Regina bounce ideas off me. Do you have a clue if she might like me back?"

Was she back in junior high again? "She likes you. I know that for a fact. Be bold when she comes back. Meet her at the airport with flowers."

"Won't she think that's too presumptuous?"

"I know her well enough to say she'll love it."

"Any particular flowers?"

She smiled at the man, thinking she would have preferred someone a little more alpha in the romance department. Who was she kidding? She would have liked a little romance even if it was delivered in a self-conscious fashion. "I'll leave that up to you."

"Roses." Max offered from underneath the table with a wink. "Chicks love them."

David pushed back from the table in surprise. "Who said that?"

"Ah, that was me." Nala forced a laugh. "It's a ventriloquism trick I do sometimes."

Her drink arrived. She took a hearty sip and sighed. At least that was going her way.

David fiddled with his tea, then gave her a curious look. "You're not driving?"

"Elvin dropped me off. It seems like this latest mission might have been a bit too much for my vintage automobile. Not sure if I can get her fixed here or tow her back home. He'll pick me up when I text him."

"That's nice. I hope someday Regina and I can be a great couple like you and Elvin. You're always helping one another, and then there's all that bantering."

She'd already explained, once, that they weren't a couple. People see what they want to see, which reminded her of the mouse incident, because of which both she and Elvin thought David might have had a glimmer of interest in her "Why did you dispose of the mice for me?"

He raised his eyebrows. "It's what we men do. That's why you ladies keep us around."

If that were the case, there were some men who needed to step up on rodent disposal. "Yes, I knew that. Just testing you."

"Any interesting cases waiting for you in Indianapolis?"

As far as she knew, nothing unusual. There were the usual date history searches. She finished a few from Regina's place. "There's a woman who wants me to locate her glass eye. It was stolen."

"Won't that be hard?"

"Shouldn't be. She knows who took it."

David gave a sage nod. "That should be easy."

That's how most of the cases started. To be fair, some *were* easy. Most weren't because whoever hired her forgot to mention pertinent facts. "We'll see."

The food arrived, and Nala slipped Max the extra quesadilla she bought. It looked like they were not getting their lunch bought for them, which was a good thing. Ashlee's parents insisted on giving her a hefty check. It just might pay for lunch, fix her car, and possibly net her some extra spyware.

Life was good.

The End

A Bark in the Night

By

M K Scott

Chapter One

A GROAN ESCAPED the silent watcher as the girl pulled out a bunch of keys to unlock the front door. The dog that had been sitting now silently stood, his ears alert, his head slowly swinging side to side as he emitted a low growl.

"Damn it." He hadn't counted on a dog. Who takes a dog with them to an office building anyhow? He could have knocked down the girl and grabbed the keys, and finally made it into the building. He'd spent the last six months trying to enter the place.

The few remaining offices weren't open to the public. He'd even donned delivery outfits and tried to get buzzed in. All he managed to discover was no one in the building had water delivered or even a pizza. Usually, he received no reply when he buzzed. It could be that the buzzer didn't work. The building itself was circa 1930s and only the bottom floor was stores, while the rest were apartments or offices.

That would have worked fine if there was an actual store on the first floor instead of empty rooms. He'd considered breaking in, but he'd most likely get caught and end up back in the slammer. Something he'd prefer to avoid since he had more enemies inside than he did out. Now, he'd have to rethink the situation. Once the girl and her dog entered the building, he tucked his hands into his jacket pocket to feel the short length of pipe he'd hidden there. A man had to protect himself, but as a felon, a gun would automatically earn a huge fine and possibly incarceration. Things he wanted to avoid.

Hands still in pockets, he strolled in the direction of Monument Circle. Sweat dotted his face due to the early heat wave. He could have pulled off his sweatshirt, but the hoodie provided conformity that made him almost invisible.

In the center of the city stood a huge war monument reaching toward the heavens as if trying to touch the departed or at least send a message they hadn't been forgotten. He couldn't remember when it had been built—sometime after the Civil War. As a kid, his grandfather had taken him there. With each war, more statues and flat memorials engraved with names appeared. He remembered fingering the names thinking the people only became important by dying. That wasn't going to be him. Nope, he'd had enough of being Toby Nobody. Once he got into the building, he'd find what was his by right and buy that sailboat he fantasized about while doing time. Might even sail around the world.

Foot and vehicle traffic picked up as he made his way to the circle. A horse-driven carriage, complete with picture-snapping tourists, passed him on one side. The harness bells jingled with the horse's movements. He was not sure why a person would even bell a horse. The animal was too large to miss. Then again, maybe the owner thought it made the experience more festive. Toby stopped and watched the slow-moving carriage. He'd never taken a carriage ride, never took a gondola ride down the canal, either. Nope, those things were for tourists or people with a lot of throwaway money. Soon, that would be him, as soon as he got rid of the obstacles.

NALA PLACED ONE hand on her hip and kept a tight grip on the leash clipped to a handsome black German shepherd mix as she surveyed the building. The stone façade building rose a good five stories, nothing compared to the other buildings looming behind it on a more visited street in Indianapolis. The morning sun revealed chipped parts of the façade and the crumbling entrance steps, exposing the underlying concrete block structure.

"The building has character." She glanced up and down the street, noticing the lack of foot traffic during the early day. The ground floor windows revealed empty rooms inside where light spots on the industrial gray carpet revealed where furniture once sat. "I was never shown a ground floor office or even one with wraparound windows." Her shoulders went up in a shrug. "It is just as well. Anyone visiting a private eye doesn't want to be on display. I probably couldn't afford it anyhow. Let's go see *our* office."

The dog gave a bark as if he understood. Nala's straight hair swung into her face as she bent to pat the animal. "That's right, Max. It's a new start for both of us."

Max and Nala climbed the first flight of stairs in silence. By the time they reached the second flight, a young man with a dark hipster beard and arms full of labeled boxes met them.

"Hey, a dog, cool!"

A bark greeted his assessment while Nala offered her hand, then pulled it back as she realized he couldn't shake. "Hello. Do you need any help with your boxes?"

"No, I'm good. I'm sure you're not coming to see me. I'd remember if I had a beautiful woman and her equally handsome dog coming to see me."

A nervous laugh greeted his remark. Blatant flirting rattled Nala since it was difficult to pinpoint if it was sincere. Extroverts could reply with clever comebacks in a second, while people like herself struggled for an appropriate reply long after the person had left. "Yeah, right."

Instead of insisting he meant it, the man grinned. "I'm Harry Chafant. I run a mail-order business on the second floor. Didn't know there were any other businesses in the building. There are some apartments in use, though. Maybe you're here to see one of the residents."

Nala shoved her hands in her jeans pockets since she didn't know what to do with them. "Ah, I'm Nala, Nala Bonne." *Oops*, she had lost a chance to try out her new name. "I'll be opening my business on the third floor. Max," she gestured to her dog, "and I are going up to check out the office."

"Really?" Harry drew out the word, and his smile grew bigger. "Today must be my lucky day. I'm headed to the post office, but when I get back I'd love to show you around."

"Thanks, but I've already seen the building." Regret stabbed her as she watched the man's smile slip. No good would come out of being too friendly to her neighbors. Even if they did hit it off, eventually they'd break up and she'd peer out her door every time a woman got buzzed in, wondering if it was her replacement. Still, she didn't want to sound unfriendly. She held up one hand. "See ya around."

"Yeah," Harry agreed and continued to descend the stairs.

If her best friend, Karly, had witnessed the scene, she'd take Nala to task, telling her she shot down another perfectly good prospect. Maybe she had, but she also avoided a messy emotional entanglement and the possibility of placing another crack in her heart. Some women threw themselves into the dating game with all the intensity of a bullfighter. A failed romance never seemed to get them down. They would just move on to the next guy. The most amazing thing about it was that there was always a next guy. In her experience, most men never passed her father's background investigation test. Oh, the joys of having a father in law enforcement.

On the third-floor landing, Nala withdrew her key to the office and opened the door. The entry office remained dusty and empty. The furniture fairies hadn't appeared overnight, not that she'd expected them to. A few words to her mother would have her scouring the design warehouse for office furniture, but she wouldn't mention it. This was something Nala wanted to accomplish on her own. With helpful, somewhat overprotective parents she seldom felt like she did much on her own. Even with school projects, she had felt they were more a group project.

Her father had built a circuit board that allowed an electrical circuit to run several items at once for the science fair. She, however, had wanted to grow plants and play music to them. When she didn't ace the science fair, her father demanded to know if the fair was fixed. It was obvious the circuit board was the superior project. Her petite teacher went toe to toe with her father and pointed out the circuit board was beyond the ability of a seven-year-old. A third-grader won with an experiment that showed tomato plants grew taller with regular shots of diet cola.

"Let's hit it." Nala dropped the leash and allowed Max to wander at will while she withdrew window cleaner, a rag, and some press-on letters. Her first project would be the exterior door.

"I'm not sure about the clear glass. If a person wants privacy they don't want everyone and their cousin peering in at them as they come to me to consult about a philandering husband or wife."

"Do people even do that anymore? I just thought they divorced, divvied up the stuff, and sometimes offloaded the family pet to a friend, relative, or took him for a ride in the country."

Nala blinked, knowing good and well no one else was in the office. She dropped her gaze to Max, who had his head cocked as if waiting for her answer. *No, it couldn't be.* Dogs didn't talk, at least not in a raspy baritone. She pinched herself just to be certain she wasn't dreaming. It hurt. *Maybe she just thought he said something. The best thing would be to test out her theory.* "Did your last owners divorce?"

Something must have happened to Max since she had picked him up at an animal shelter the day before he would have been put down. Grown dogs were only kept for a few days at the most. Then again, it could be she wanted Max to talk so she'd have someone to converse with. A fellow traveler in this new life she'd plotted out for herself.

"Nope." He grimaced, showing his teeth. "I made the mistake of talking again. Not the first time I've been ousted from a comfortable home. This last time I was driven from the house by my former owner holding a crucifix and calling me *devil dog*."

"Weird." She shook her head hard still not convinced she wasn't dreaming. I would have thought someone would have put you on the David Letterman show. Whoops, I keep forgetting he retired." *Was she really having a conversation with her dog?*

"You'd think that." He barked a couple of times before continuing. "You gotta remember English is my third language and some things don't translate."

"You speak three languages?"

He lifted his nose with pride. "I do. Dog, of course, the silent language of scent, and I'm reasonably conversant in English. One potential owner tried to speak to me in German. Despite my muddied bloodlines, I couldn't understand a word he said. I wanted to tell him I was born in America. I didn't, since I wasn't totally sure."

"Ah, of course." She nodded her head as if she understood. *Was there anything understandable about a talking dog*? "So, when did you start talking? Are there a lot of talking dogs out there?"

His nose dropped as he stretched out and laid his head on his paws. "All dogs talk in the accepted canine dialect, except for basenjis who do this strange yodeling thing. I haven't met one who speaks English, although most do understand it very well. They might pretend not to know phrases such as stay off the couch, not for you, or not now. They do. Even though they understand English, they freak out when I say something. Something about it being us against them, meaning your kind."

"Ah." Nala searched her mind for how she had treated Max in the few days she owned him. Had she offended him somehow by treating him like a dog? "You never answered how you came to talk."

"Oh, that." He managed a few sharp yips that resembled a laugh. "Funny story. My first owner was a close-mouthed male. Not one to share his feelings or general observations about life. While this didn't bother me all that much, it was an entirely different story for his girlfriend, who happened to be a witch. She always fixed extra scrambled eggs and bacon for me when she visited, so I liked her. Anyhow, one day, she says to the man, 'If you don't talk to me, then your dog will.'"

"Just like that?"

"Took me a while to become a good conversationalist. At the time, I was so excited I voiced every thought." He lifted his head enough to display a doggy grin. "Imagine a constant litany of me listing everything I saw. Tree, grass, dog poop from the poodle two houses down, smells like she likes me. After all, she left it in front of my house. Well, you get the idea."

"Irritating."

"Yep, I discovered immediately that while people yack non-stop, they don't appreciate a talkative dog, especially my first owner who didn't even make the effort to talk to his girlfriend. One day, she was gone. Not sure if they agreed to separate. I just noticed the house smelled less like the sandalwood incense she always burned. After that, I got relocated, too."

"Where?"

"A family with kids. They had a little boy I adored. He wasn't that good at walking so he often hung onto me when he was unstable. It was only natural that I tried to encourage him. His parents were worried about his developing psyche and the dangers of believing a dog could talk. They thought I was a bad influence." Max stood, paced to the hallway and returned to his original place before circling and flopping back down on the floor.

"That's too bad about the kid. I'm not sure what I'll do with a talking dog."

A foul smell permeated the air. "Sorry." Max offered her an apologetic expression. "The Chinese food you gave me yesterday doesn't agree with me. I love it, though. Besides, stress has that effect, too."

Her intention had been to get a dog for companionship. Karly, who worked at the shelter, had emailed her pictures of dogs that would be put down. *Talk about guilt.* Even worse, when they met for lunch, she'd talk about the abandoned dogs, giving them names and listing their idiosyncrasies. Nala pointed out more than once that if Karly wanted someone to adopt a dog it was better not to mention things such as its tendency to rip up anything vaguely chewable or its midnight howling. Karly insisted people had to enter relation-ships with open eyes.

As if that would ever work. There was a reason woman shoved themselves into shapewear, piled on the makeup, and clipped on hair extensions. Men didn't want reality, and she was sure women didn't either. On occasion, when they needed a reality check, they'd hire an investigator. She'd specialize in date research. No woman wanted to go on a date with an online prospect or even the cousin of a co-worker and end up battered, broke or, worse, dead.

"We'll have to limit your intake to the weekends. Can't have you scaring off the clients with your toxic farts."

A hopeful gleam appeared in Max's eyes as his ears pitched for-ward. "Do you mean you're going to keep me?"

"Why not?"

"The talking usually scares people off, but Karly assured me you'd be okay with it. Since you're into magic, psychic skills, and all that." His long tail wagged, hitting the floor. The empty room magnified the sound.

"Karly knew? The woman who never believes in too much information withheld the fact from me that you could speak?"

"She never told you she didn't like Jeff, either."

Nala looked up from pecking at her cell with her index finger. "You mean you and Karly talked about my ex-boyfriend?"

Max swallowed hard. "You know, I could be an immense help around the detective agency."

"How so?"

"Scent. I can tell if people are lying or not by their scent."

She shook her head, imagining how well a large German shepherd mix sniffing them would go over. "I'm pretty sure my future clients and suspects wouldn't go for you sticking your nose in their crotch."

"Please." He managed a huff. "I have excellent scent ability. The nose in the crotch thing is something dogs do just for fun. It's a game we like to play with humans. If you didn't react so strongly, then it wouldn't be as hilarious."

Author Notes

A Bark in The Night (the first book) was written after many requests from the local readers for a story set in Indianapolis. I certainly knew the town and surrounding areas. Many of the businesses and streets mentioned in the story do exist. The characters and the very lovable Max are entirely my creation.

Come and visit Indianapolis some time. You might be surprised at its several first-class restaurants and venues. I even have an adorable bed and breakfast to recommend too, The Nestle Inn.

Love to see you. In the meantime, stay in touch via my newsletter. Sign up at www.morgankwyatt.com.

Subscribers find out about exclusive freebies, contests, and personal appearances.

If you feel like writing a review, please do.

Reading takes you to your happy place.

MK Scott

www.morgankwyatt.com